To everyone who dreams of being kissed under the mistletoe.

Tinsel in Telluride

HAYDEN LOCKE

Chapter One

LEIGH

My lies are catching up with me.

Well, one in particular.

In my defense, I've had a damn good reason for not telling the truth about my son's parentage. But now my worlds are colliding and there's nothing I can do to stop the inevitable catastrophe that lies ahead.

"Leigh?" Willow waves her hand in front of my face, the obnoxious bells sewn into the sleeves of her festive sweater jingling with every move.

"Hmm?" I look up from the popcorn I somehow got roped into stringing for a Christmas party I absolutely don't want to attend. If it wasn't for the incessant desire to give my son a normal childhood, I would be avoiding it like I do every year. But alas, here I am.

My best friend, who also happens to be my boss, narrows her scrutinizing gaze and repeats the question I conveniently ignored seconds ago. "I asked about the Renegade Hearts expansions. Is everything in order to be finished on schedule?"

Fuck.

It's not.

But what am I supposed to say? *Hey, I've got twenty-nine of the thirty teams all onboarded and ready to start building their individual chapters, but remember that one-night stand almost two years ago that left me knocked up? Yeah? Well, I kinda lied when I said I knew who the baby daddy was. The truth is, it's one of two men and now that lie has come back to haunt me like the Ghost of Christmas Past, only this time he's a gorgeous.Italian in a Tom Ford suit who will absolutely kill me when he finds out.*

Absolutely not.

I twirl the needle between my fingers, before nonchalantly stabbing another piece of popcorn and do what I do best when backed into a corner—deflect. "Define in order."

Willow rolls her eyes, following it up with a slow shake of her head as she focuses on the separating tinsel. "Let me guess, the Monarch Chapter?"

Willow always jokes that I'm the perceptive one in our little friend trio, while Indie is the charismatic one, and she is the wise one. But it's clear she hasn't missed the subtle clues over the last nine months that I'm less than thrilled to be working with the Monarchs—specifically their owner.

Eight months ago, I was ecstatic when the MLB Commissioner announced the league would become an official partner with Willow's philanthropy, Renegade Hearts. The partnership includes expanding Hearts' Chapters to each team in the league and has opened so many incredible avenues to help kids, who have lost one or both parents, cope and move forward.

As someone who lost her parents as a teenager, I love the mission behind what we do. As Willow's partner and CFO, though, I'm selfishly hating that I've become the go-to person for establishing these chapters.

Chest full of shame, I sigh, press my lips together and nod, confirming Willow's astute observation.

Willow cocks a brow and, like any good best friend, digs a little deeper. "Does this have anything to do with a six-foot-four, charming ex-baseball-player-turned-owner that has decided he's going to head up Monarch Hearts himself instead of handing it off to his team?"

See what I mean? Perceptive.

"Maybe," I answer too quickly, my voice going high at the end.

"Leighton Bennett."

Fuck.

She full named me.

The only time Willow York full names you is when she's absolutely done with your bullshit.

Not only that, but she used my parent's last name. The name I changed in order to distance myself from everything that happened in Shady Grove.

"Fine." I drop the popcorn in my hand to the table and look away from her prying gaze. "Yes, it has to do with him, but I promise to have everything up and running with his chapter by the end of the year deadline."

"It's December twentieth," Willow deadpans, and I wince.

"I know."

"Most people don't work the last week of the year."

"I know."

"And we need everything to the commissioner's office by the end of the—"

"I know, Wills," I snap, making the mistake of looking up.

The hurt I see flash in Willow's eyes guts me.

This deal for Renegade Hearts is really important to her. It's important to me. I hate that my own bullshit is the reason it's not done yet.

"I'll get it finished."

"Will you?" she asks, not as my best friend but as my boss. "Because if you need me to assign this one team to someone else, I can."

"No, it's fine," I reassure her. "This is my mess, and I'm going to figure it out."

Or die trying.

I promised myself when I found out I was pregnant with Zach that I wasn't going to let my pregnancy or the circumstances get in the way of my future. And I have done just that. I've made sure Renegade Hearts continues to grow while Willow has taken a leave of absence to be a present owner for the Renegades baseball team. Our summer camp is thriving. And Zach is growing into the sweetest little boy.

I've done all that.

Me.

I will figure this out too.

Her tense brows soften, and she offers me a warm smile. "Are you going to tell me what happened between the two of you?"

No.

Yes.

I should. I really should. Willow has been there for me through every up and down in my life for the better part of fifteen years. But if I tell her the truth, then it makes it real, and I've rather enjoyed the space of denial I've created for myself.

See? Deflection at its finest.

"What's going on between who?" Indiana Lewis, the third wheel to our friendship tricycle, slides into the seat next to me and pops a piece of popcorn in her mouth. Picking up a strip of tinsel, she ties it to the end of her thick black braid, making it a fashion statement in a way only Indie can.

God, I hate that stuff. I don't know who thought it was a good idea to throw loose strands of glitter on trees, but it just gets everywhere and makes a mess.

Indie glances between Willow and me, her pointed gaze landing on Willow. "Also, your boyfriend's best friend is sneaking Zachary candy to introduce him to the pretty volunteers."

All three of us swivel our heads and watch as my almost two-year-old son teeters up to a volunteer and proceeds to point to the Renegades Ace pitcher, and says, "Cawson."

The pretty brunette volunteer, who looks like she's dressed for a night out at a club and not to set up a kid's Christmas party, falls to one knee and coos at Zach before looking up at Carson with hearts in her eyes. "Is he your son?"

I roll my eyes and yell across the banquet hall at Willow's boyfriend. "Bishop, get your teammate in line. And Carson, stop using my son as your pickup line."

Carson lifts my sweet boy in his arms and twirls him in a circle. Zach's laughs echo, making my heart melt. It's a stark reminder that he needs this. I can't keep him locked away in order to protect him. He needs people in his life that he can count on. And these people are good people. People I trust. They aren't going to leave us.

Maybe if I say it enough, I'll finally believe it.

Carson laughs and sets my son down, giving our table a shrug. "Don't hate the player, hate the game."

He makes a show of handing Zach his reward, a piece of chocolate, and ruffles his too long blonde hair. "Your mom's no fun, you know that?"

"I used to be fun," I mutter, mostly to myself. Now my thoughts revolve around remembering to make an appointment to get my son's hair cut and worrying if he pooped today or not.

Indie chuckles beside me. "Yeah, then you let your vagina become a bat-infested cave instead of the cave of wonders."

"It hasn't been that long," I counter, picking up my needle and stabbing another piece of popcorn.

But it has.

Almost two years and nine months, to be exact.

"No, no, we're not getting sidetracked by Leigh's lack of sex life." Willow's gaze narrows in my direction. "Back to business. Why is it we're not allowed to talk about whatever it is that happened between you and Luca?"

"Oh, yes, do tell, because I've got a bet going with Bishop, and I can't wait to rub it in his face when he's wrong." Indie leans forward and pulls the bowl of popcorn in front of her. She rests her elbows on the table and brings a piece to her mouth like she is just waiting for the show to begin.

Willow scoffs. "You've got bets going with my boyfriend?"

"So many bets." Indie wiggles her eyebrows, taunting Willow, who she knows can't stand not knowing anything and everything. "But that's not the point."

"We'll put a pin in that," Willow concedes and shifts her gaze back to me. "The point is, what's going on with you and Luca? And will this affect Renegade Hearts?"

"Seriously, I don't understand why you wouldn't want to work with that tree of a man and then maybe climb him and break your self-imposed celibacy."

"Weeelll," I draw out the word and drop my shoulders in defeat, "that's sort of the problem. I've already climbed that tree."

"Wait, you slept with Luca?" Willow gasps at the same time Indie throws up her hands, sending tinsel flying everywhere and shouts, "I knew it! Bishop owes me fifty bucks."

Heat fills my cheeks as I pick the tinsel from my hair. "That's not the problem, though."

"Go on," Indie singsongs.

"Luca may or may not be The Scum of the Upper Peninsula."

"What!" they both exclaim.

I drag my hand down my face. There isn't a single part of me that wants to relive this.

Luca's sister Gianna was my first friend when we moved to Shady Grove. She was my best friend. We did everything together. Until the day Luca accused me of stealing a family heirloom in front of the entire town.

I still don't know how the locket got in my bag, but I know it was him. He all but told me it was. From that point on, no one wanted their children to be associated with the delinquent of Shady Grove.

That included Gianna.

When I showed up at our boarding school in the fall, Willow and Indie were there to pick up the pieces. I told them the story, but never his name in fear that they, or their society families, would side with him and the Donati name, and I'd lose them too.

They got me through the school year, even coming up with the nickname for Luca to make me laugh. But every summer until I left for college, I'd go home and was reminded just how unwanted I was in our little town.

And it was all thanks to him.

I glance around the room to make sure there isn't anyone listening in on our conversation. Most of the volunteers have finished setting up. A few members of the team that agreed to help with the party are all circled up with my son in the corner, trying to teach him to play catch with a crumpled up piece of wrapping paper.

Willow is the first to recover from her shock and rapid-fires a line of questions. "Luca is the SCUP? How did we not know this? Why didn't you tell us sooner? Is that how he knew your name back at spring training? Wait, when did you sleep with him?"

My gut roils with anxiety, but I answer them in succession. "Yes. I didn't want you to know. He definitely recognized me, and almost two years and nine months ago."

And then I wait.

And wait.

It takes a moment, but Willow pieces it together first.

"No," she gasps, bringing her hands to cover her mouth.

"What did I miss?" Indie asks, following Willow's gaze to my son.

"Oh, fuck."

Now she gets it.

"Luca might be Zach's father," I admit softly, my voice shaky.

It's the first time I've ever said the words out loud. They cut deeper than I expected, but also bring a sense of relief that I'm not the only keeper of this secret anymore.

"So, The Scum of the Upper Peninsula is also the Scum of the Upper East Side?" Indie clarifies and I wince, wishing it wasn't true.

I'm also realizing we need to diversify the way we nickname shitty men.

"Not exactly," I explain, shame washing over me. "He *might* be The Scum of the Upper East side, but he also might not be."

They're both silent, eyes zeroed on me, waiting for further explanation.

"Remember that hospice fundraiser you didn't want to go to and sent me instead?" I say to Willow.

She nods. "It's not that I didn't want to go. I was sick."

"Sure, we'll go with that." We both know it's a bald-faced lie. Before Bishop came along, my bestie hated public speaking and schmoozing donors. It didn't matter that her name did all the convincing. She frequently pawned events off on me.

"Either way," I continue, "that night Luca was at the fundraiser."

"And what you fell on his dick?"

I roll my eyes. "So eloquent, Inds, but essentially yes."

What really happened was I didn't say no when he asked me to dance, because after a few too many glasses of champagne, I had every intention of telling him all the reasons he really was the Scum of the Upper Peninsula. Which I did. Then he responded with how incredibly sexy that was. The next thing I knew, we were in a closet at the end of the hallway, fucking up against a vending machine. Skittles falling out as we both came brings a whole new meaning to taste the rainbow.

"Does he know?" Willow murmurs, trying and failing to keep the hint of judgment from her voice.

I wince internally. She doesn't mean anything malicious by it. She's come to care for Luca after he helped her and Bishop out this past spring. If it wasn't for him, the two of them likely wouldn't be together. Which blows my mind. The Luca Donati I know doesn't do anything without an agenda.

Still, I'm the asshole here, no doubt.

"No. I didn't tell him. I don't know for sure if Zach is his, or if he belongs to the guy I hooked up with from the club the weekend before."

Though it would be par for the course if Luca were the father.

My entire life has been a testament of taking lemons and making lemonade. Why should this be any different?

When everyone in my hometown thought I was a delinquent—I found my friends at boarding school. When my parents died in a tragic accident—I helped start a nonprofit for children who've lost their parents. I got knocked up and couldn't marry the guy my grandparents wanted in order to get back into the good graces of society—I'm thriving being a single mom doing it all on my own.

In short, I wouldn't be surprised if Luca Donati turns out to be the father of my son. I'm just not sure how the hell I'm supposed to make lemonade with that.

Willow furrows her brow, and I already know what my glass-half-full friend is going to say.

"I'm still having a hard time reconciling Luca is the same guy who accused you of stealing."

It's the same argument I've been making in the confines of my mind since seeing him at spring training. Because she's right. He doesn't seem like he's the same guy.

But tigers can't shed their stripes. And I've been burned too many times by the Donati family to believe he hasn't got ulterior motives.

"So, what now?" Indie asks. "Are you going to tell him?"

I shrug and pick at the skin at the corner of my nail in a futile attempt to avoid their stares. "Now I figure out how to work with him and then we move on."

"For what it's worth, I think you should tell him." Willow presses her lips together, and I get the feeling it's the only thing stopping her from saying more.

"Of course you do," I scoff, at the same time Indie rasps a high pitched, "Really?"

Willow shrugs sheepishly, twirling a piece of her golden blonde hair around her finger. "I'm just saying. I think Luca will surprise you. Plus, we see so many kids come through Renegade Hearts, wishing they had both of their parents. You have the opportunity to give that to Zach."

A lighthearted laugh escapes me, but it's nothing but a cover for the hurt at my failure to give Zach the one thing he deserves.

A proper family.

When I found out I was pregnant, I'd never even considered Luca as part of Zach's life. It would be too messy. Too complicated. And that's assuming he's his father. But since running into him eight months ago, I can't say the notion hasn't crossed my mind. Usually, it's when I'm sleep deprived and overwhelmed. Then I get some coffee in my system, and I remember I hate him, firmly squashing the wayward thought.

"I don't think he's lacking father figures," Indie disagrees, gesturing to where Bishop and his teammates are still entertaining Zach.

"I'm not sure that's a valid argument." Willow chuckles. "I've seen the questionable decisions those men make on a daily basis. Again, all I'm saying is maybe use this time working with him to get to know him." She reaches across the table and takes my hand in hers, giving it a gentle squeeze. "Then you can decide if telling him is what's best for Zach."

"I'll think about it." It's not concrete, but it's the best answer I can give while my heart is trying to reconcile that I have no choice but to face this. "But are you sure there isn't any way I can have until after the first of the year to get this done?"

The holidays are already hard. The last thing I need is Luca to make them worse.

Willow winces, catching my apprehension. "I wish. But it's my ass if it's not on the commissioner's desk by the thirty-first. So, no."

Indie throws her arm around me and rests her head on my shoulder. Looking up at me, she bats her eyelashes sweetly. "Do you want us to hold your hand while you call him? At least you can't fall on his dick from across the country."

God, I love the way these women can be angry for me, challenge me, fight for me, then make me laugh when all I want to do is cry in the span of the same five minutes.

"No," I huff, rolling my eyes. "I'll do it tonight after we get home. It'll still be early in Los Angeles after I get Zach to bed."

"Fine." Indie slumps back into her chair like I've just ruined her day. "But the offer still stands."

"You just want to be a fly on the wall."

She winks. "You know I live for the drama."

Well, there will definitely be no shortage of that.

Chapter Two

LEIGH

Anxiety makes a permanent home in the base of my stomach as I glance at the baby monitor on the kitchen island for the millionth time. If Zach moves—just a little bit or even whimpers—then I have an excuse to go to him and not make this call.

Of course he doesn't.

The freaking traitor.

Doesn't he know his mom is on the verge of a panic attack and could really use an out right about now?

As swiftly as the anger hits me, guilt slices just as deep. None of this is his fault, and it's not his job to save me. He's an innocent bystander in this mess.

But also, I didn't ask for this.

Sure. Some people would argue I had sex with Luca, so it's my own damn fault. To them, I raise a silent middle finger and say I didn't know antibiotics could negate birth control for a number of days after finishing them. Was that irresponsible of me? Maybe. But I did my best to make sure this didn't happen.

I'm not saying I don't love my son. That sweet little boy who is obsessed with horses and afraid of his own shadow is my freaking world.

That doesn't mean there aren't moments that brand me as human and make me feel like a horrible mother.

This is one of them.

The kicker is, I know one day he is going to grow up and ask about this. And when he does, I need to be able to tell him I did the right thing. I told the truth. I admitted my mistakes and owned my downfalls.

For him.

I'm doing this for him.

But not without a little liquid courage.

I swivel off my stool, round the small island, and grab the bottle of Zinfandel from the fridge. For a split second, I contemplate drinking straight from the bottle. Then I remember the last time I did so and immediately grab a glass from the cupboard.

Hangovers suck when you have a toddler.

Pouring myself a generous amount, I return to my spot and double check that my son still hasn't moved.

He hasn't.

The clock on my phone reads eight, which means it's five o'clock in Los Angeles. Maybe if I wait five more minutes, he'll be out of the office for the day, and I can just leave a message.

Dread coils inside me, like a snake lying in wait, as I hover my thumb over Luca's number.

I could make excuses all night if I needed to, but that doesn't help me, Willow, or Zach.

It's now or never.

Forcing my finger down, I wait. It rings three times before Luca's deep, velvet baritone echoes through the speaker.

"I was beginning to wonder if you were ever going to call."

Like a Pavlovian response, his voice takes me back to that night and all the filthy things he uttered while I was on my knees.

Fuck, Little Thief, you take my cock so well.

The whispered praises in my ear as I came all over his thick cock.

You're such a good fucking girl.

Nope. I can't do this.

Because this is the part of the truth I conveniently left out when I told my friends about Luca—mostly because I'm ashamed to admit it even to myself. As much as I hate him for what he did when I was young, the moment I hear his voice, I can't forget the way he made my body sing. It was the same when I saw him at spring training this past March.

Panties instantly wet.

Which is a problem, because even if what started as a hate fuck turned into the kind of passion you only read about in romance novels, none of it was real.

It can't be.

Not then. And not now.

I swallow hard past the knot in my throat and clench my shaking hands in an attempt to ground myself and remember why I called in the first place.

Monarch Hearts.

Not my cobweb filled pussy.

Make a plan.

Don't give in to his devilish charm.

End the call.

Simple as that.

"Hello, Mr. Donati," I say, proud of the way I'm able to keep my voice steady despite the overwhelming urge to vomit.

"Mr. Donati, is it?" Luca chuckles. "I'm fairly certain we're past formalities, Ms. James."

Why? Because I know what you sound like when you come?

The snark is on the tip of my tongue, but I somehow manage to keep it to myself. "I'm calling about setting up some time for us to meet and discuss the Monarch Hearts' chapter. Your assistant let me know you'd be handling it directly, and I should coordinate with you."

There's a beat of silence, and I think maybe the call has been disconnected when Luca finally speaks. "Okay. Then let's figure out a time you can come out here after the first of the year, so we can get everything set up."

"Yeah, that's not going to work," I snap, followed by a wince as I remember this is my job, and he is the owner of the Monarchs, not just my maybe-baby-daddy.

I sip my wine and let out a weary sigh. "The commissioner wants everything on his desk by the thirty-first. I don't need to come out to Los Angeles. Most of the other chapters I was able to get squared away over a few phone calls. The in-person stuff will come later when we get the rec centers built."

"Hmm," Luca muses and I brace for what I'm sure is going to be a bullshit answer. "Unfortunately, that's not going to work for me. I'm already out of town, and I won't be back until after the holidays."

"You won't have access to your phone or email?" I ask, grasping at straws. "I could just coordinate with your assistant."

"As Roy told you, I'm going to be handling this myself, and no, reception will be spotty here at best." I don't miss the hint of smugness in his tone. "You're lucky I was able to take this call at all."

The bastard knows what he's doing. I'd bet money he's retaliating because I didn't answer his call the week after we hooked up. Then again, after he saw me at spring training. Or the ten other times he's tried since.

Shit.

Willow's going to kill me.

Our first big partnership and I'm already fucking it up.

"Please, Luca." I soften my voice, apparently no longer above begging.

"I need to get this done for Willow by the end of the year. You know how important this is to her."

"I know exactly how important this is to *both* of you. Which begs the question, why have you waited until the last minute to do this?"

"You just happened to be the last team on the docket," I lie, hating the way it's become so easy to do so, but I also don't like the way he emphasized the word *both*. Like he's trying to make sure I know this is about me too.

If only he knew the truth.

"I'm sure." Luca's voice drips with sarcasm, and I can picture the sexy way he cocks his brow when he's caught me in a lie.

Tell me you want me, Little Thief.

I hate you.

Which only makes you want me more.

Damn it.

I can't think about that right now.

"Listen," I implore. "What can we do so this gets done in time? Willow can't afford to be in hot water with the commissioner after the scandal with her father this past year."

He hesitates and I picture him chewing his lower lip the way he did just before he told me I could leave or hate fuck the shit out of him.

"Meet me in Telluride."

I blink, convinced I've misheard him. Because there's no way he just asked me to go with him on vacation. "Colorado?"

"You said you need to get this done by the end of the year. I'm in Telluride with some friends for the holidays. Come here."

"I can't just crash your vacation with your friends. Nor do I want to. You hate me, remember?"

Luca doesn't miss a beat and fires back. "I absolutely do not hate you. And don't think of it as crashing a vacation. Think of it as a work trip with a little tinsel."

"What is it with everyone and tinsel? It's not even a good Christmas decoration."

"I didn't know you were a grinch, Ms. Bennett."

"It's James and you know it," I snap. "Plus, you might not hate me, but you absolutely don't like me."

"My dick says otherwise," he mutters, and I get the feeling it wasn't a sentiment meant for my ears.

Which is too damn bad because at this point the gloves are off, and I'm not about to let it go.

"That's what this is about?" I screech, immediately regretting my choice when I see Zach stir on the monitor.

Five painfully slow seconds pass, and I watch to make sure he isn't about to wake up and choose violence. When I'm sure he's still asleep, I lower my voice and whisper yell into the phone. "You want me to come to Telluride for a freaking booty call?"

"No," he whispers back. "I want you to—Fuck, why are we whispering?"

I roll my eyes. "My son is asleep, and I don't want to wake him."

The moment the words leave my mouth, I know I fucked up.

Even more so when Luca's voice perks up. "You have a son?"

Damn it. This isn't how I meant for him to find out. Not that I had a plan. Hell, I barely decided today that I might consider telling him. And that's only because Willow made some good points about Zach deserving to know his dad, and I have a guilty conscience.

"Leigh," he presses with privileged impatience.

I huff in frustration and force a professional, per-my-last-email tone. "Yes. Which is why I can't come to Telluride just because your dick likes me."

Okay, so maybe professional went out the window a long time ago.

Luca lets out a long breath, mumbling a curse as he does, and I imagine him rolling his eyes, trying to find some semblance of order to this conversation.

Welcome to the club, buddy.

I knew this wasn't going to be easy, but I didn't expect it to be a total clusterfuck. I'm also realizing it's far too easy for my mind to fill in the blanks of what he looks like on the other end of this phone, and I don't think I like what that implies.

"That came out wrong."

I tilt my head for no one's benefit but my own. "Ya think?"

"Listen, I want you to come to Telluride so we can get everything set up for Monarch Hearts. My friends and I rented a place and there's plenty of room. I've been hoping to see you. We can get Monarch Hearts all dialed in…" His voice trails off like there's more he wants to say.

When he doesn't, I offer him a resounding, "This is a bad idea."

For so many reasons. Primarily because I don't trust him, but I also don't think I can trust myself around him.

And what does he mean by he's been hoping to see me?

No. I stop myself from going down that rabbit hole.

Professional is best. We can meet in his office. At the stadium. Anywhere that isn't a vacation home in the mountains. With snow. Real snow. Not the stuff we get here in New York City that covers the spaces between buildings. Snow like back in Michigan that sweeps across fields and mountains, sticking to every towering tree.

I never thought I'd be homesick for a place that ruined so much of my life.

"Leigh, I also wanted to apologize for…" He stops himself, searching for words, and I find myself holding my breath as I wait for him to finish. "…for what happened back home."

My jaw drops. You could tell me pigs were flying outside my window, and I'd believe you sooner than I'd believe the words coming out of this man's mouth.

I sit up a little straighter on my stool, anger coursing through me to the point my body feels like it's vibrating. "Donatis don't apologize."

Those were the words he told me ten years ago when I was nothing but a scared fifteen-year-old, trying to get her life back to normal.

"Please, Leigh." Desperation, like a prayer, laces his tone, and I loathe the way it pulls at my heartstrings.

"If you have something to say, you can say it right now," I declare, standing my ground.

"It's really something I'd rather do in person."

"Luca," I snap, my rage getting the better of me. "I can't just leave on such short notice. I don't have a sitter, and even if I did, I can't leave my almost two-year-old just because you want me to. We have to work together, but that doesn't mean we have to fix everything between us all in one go."

"He's two?"

Shit.

Shit. Shit. Shit.

Panic grips my spine and I worry my lower lip, knowing damn well Luca isn't stupid.

Why do I keep slipping up with him?

My mind scrambles for something, anything, to say that isn't *yup*, with a sarcastic pop of the P at the end, but nothing formulates.

"Bring him with you," Luca offers, his tone even and giving nothing away.

"You—you want me to bring my son to a work trip in Telluride?" I stammer, trying to work out how much he's figured out and what he's thinking.

"If that's what it takes to get you here, then yes." He pauses and I hear the faint sound of people cheering in the background before he continues,

"I've spent far too many years regretting my actions, and the last time we spent more than a few minutes together, there wasn't exactly much talking going on."

I wince. "Please don't remind me."

I've already relived it multiple times during this phone call and will likely have to take care of myself later.

"The house is big enough that you'll have your own room," he continues, ignoring my protests. "We can work on getting Monarch Hearts set up. Then we can talk, and you and your son can leave and be home for Christmas."

"This is insane," I whisper, mostly to myself.

"Please, Leigh," he rasps.

Fuck.

Why do I have to be a sucker for guys who beg?

Still, it's on the tip of my tongue to tell him I can't, when my eyes fall to the little boy cuddling with his stuffed horse.

What if Zach is a Donati?

Was Willow right? Do I need to give him a chance?

What if Luca really has changed, and this is him making amends?

I know the right answer, but fuck if that's what I want to do.

"Luca, if I do this, there's something you need to know—"

"Leigh," he cuts me off, "I was an accounting major. I'm good with numbers."

"I know but—"

"We'll talk about it in Telluride."

His voice gives away none of his emotions, but mine does. It wobbles as I try to confess. "This isn't…You might—"

"In. Telluride." Luca punctuates each word, and this time I can hear every bit of the agitation he's trying to hide.

I chew my lower lip to the point of breaking skin, the copper taste of my blood flooding my tastebuds. I can't believe I'm considering this. It's crazy. Insane. The exact opposite of everything I've ever done. I'm not the impulsive one. That's Indie. Nor am I the whimsical one. That's Willow. I'm the logical one. The one that holds our little group together with reason and calm. I always have a plan.

This is not part of the plan.

Then again, neither was Zach, and he's the best thing that ever happened to me.

"Fine." I sigh, praying I don't regret this manic moment of bravery on behalf of my son. "On one condition."

"Name it."

"Zach and I get our own place to stay." If I'm going to do this, we need a place that we can retreat to the moment this all becomes too much—for me or for Zach.

"Done."

"Really?" I ask, my voice cracking. "That simple?"

"I meant what I said. I want to apologize." The sincerity in his voice makes me think he's serious. "And it seems we have more to talk about as well."

Then he goes and ruins it with snark.

I roll my eyes and sigh with hardly any confidence left.

Because he's not wrong.

"Okay," I agree. "But for the record, this is strictly business. No more talk about your dick."

Luca chuckles. "I swear not to mention my dick unless it's you who asks about him."

"I won't," I grind out.

"Good, because I don't fuck thieves."

My jaw drops as he ends the call.

The fucking audacity of this man.

But as his words sink in, I'm smacked by the weight of them.

Fifteen years ago, I might not have been the thief he accused me of being, but if Zach is his son, I've become the worst kind of thief.

Because, unlike jewelry, time can never be replaced.

Chapter Three

LUCA

I'm not sure how long I stare at the fireplace after I hang up the phone with Leigh. My thoughts race and I'm torn between wanting to punch in the drywall of the rental house and calling her back to demand answers.

A son.

She has a son.

I might have a son.

Why didn't she tell me?

What does he look like?

Is he mine?

If he's not mine, whose is he?

Was the sex so bad that she had to sleep with someone else so she could forget me?

No. I'm fucking amazing in bed.

If there's another guy, he definitely came before me.

But what does that make me?

The rebound?

Sloppy seconds?

What if he is mine?

Do I want him to be?

Fuck.

"You wanna explain what that was about and why, instead of answering, me you're staring at the fireplace like it's going to explode?"

"Huh?" I look up and find my twin standing in the doorway of the room we dubbed the makeshift office. Really, it's an additional living room, but when you're staying with three other owners of professional teams for the holidays, two of which are still in season, a quiet place to work is necessary.

"How the hell do you do that?" I ask as Enzo enters the room and plops down on the couch next to me.

"What?" My twin lifts his hand and examines his fingernails like the pretentious asshole he is, pretending he doesn't know exactly what I'm talking about.

I arch a scrutinizing brow in his direction, and he chuckles.

Ever since we were kids, Enzo's had the uncanny ability to just appear out of nowhere. It suits him as the quiet and contemplative half of this dynamic duo, but damn if it isn't both unnerving and utterly annoying.

"Usually, I'd say I'm just the stealthy twin, but this time I absolutely made my presence known. You just were too lost in the conversation you were having."

Was I?

"Now you wanna tell me who you just invited to Christmas?"

Fuck.

"No one." I lock my eyes back on the fire, hoping he'll drop it.

Of course, ever the perceptive jackass, he doesn't. "Really? Because it sure as hell sounded like you did."

"She'll be in the guest house. None of you will even know she's here." It's a terrible plan. Even I know that, but I couldn't let the opportunity pass me by.

Leigh Bennett—James now, I remind myself—is my path to redemption.

And maybe my future.

If there's even a chance that little boy is my son, I deserve to know.

"Oh, so it's a she. Alright, we're getting somewhere." Enzo tilts his head and offers me a mischievous grin. He sits up a little straighter and steeples his fingers together. "Though I'm pretty sure we have rules about bringing guests, especially women, to Bucket List Christmas."

"Fuck the rules."

Enzo chuckles, enjoying this turn of events far too much.

Every year, me, my brother and our two best friends—Holt and Bash—leave our respective cities and teams in California to meet up for Christmas. The rules of the trip are simple: we go to a new location, picked by one of us from the bucket list of our lost comrade, Jack. It's our way of honoring him and making sure our little family gets together at least once a year.

I added the additional rule of *no women* because of Bash and his fucking accent. It doesn't matter where in the world Christmas takes us, that smooth talking bastard always ends up bringing strays back to the house to celebrate with us. Any other time of year I wouldn't care, but Christmas is just for the four of us. The only exception being if there is an intent to shackle a ring on the fourth finger.

I can't believe my own damn rules are coming back to bite me in the ass.

Honestly, when I made them, I petitioned for vows to be exchanged before ever letting any woman ruin what we have.

That was before today.

Initially, the plan was to help Leigh out, make sure Monarch Hearts got set up in time, prove I'm no longer an asshole, and apologize for my crimes. She'd be here a day or two—tops. Maybe we'd have a repeat of that night in the vending machine closet, with the opportunity for future nights together when we were on the same coast. Afterwards, Leigh would be back home before Christmas, and the guys would've never even known she was here.

Now I'm forsaking every word I ever said—every rule I ever made—in order to get Leigh and that little boy to Telluride.

Because if he's mine, then there's not a chance I'm missing another Christmas.

Or birthday.

Or future school plays.

I'm done missing everything.

My hands fist in my lap. The urge to punch something back in full force.

"She has a kid," I admit. Only because he's my brother—my twin. He knows me better than anyone else. If there's anyone who can talk this through objectively, it's him.

Enzo cocks a brow, his interest clearly piqued. "And who is this mysterious *she*?"

I don't immediately answer but relax when his amused expression gives way to concern. "Leigh Bennett."

His pompous expression slips, and Enzo presses his lips together, holding back a laugh. "This wouldn't happen to be the same Leigh Bennett you accused of stealing our mother's priceless necklace, would it? Who is now Leigh James, the CFO of Renegade Hearts?"

"Yeah," I confirm reluctantly, bracing for the ribbing I know is coming.

"The same Leigh James you let hate fuck you at the hospice gala because you were in your feels and had too much tequila."

"One and the same."

"And she has a kid."

"He's two," I deadpan.

It takes Enzo all of two point five seconds to put the pieces together. His eyes go wide and he whispers a less than eloquent, "Oh fuck."

You know it's bad when you've reduced Lorenzo Donati to profanities.

I press my lips together and nod. "Exactly."

"Are you sure he's yours?"

"I don't know."

"Why didn't you just ask her?"

"I—" My gaze tracks to the large floor-to-ceiling windows, watching the snow fall in fat fluffy clumps as I try to find a way to admit my thoughts without making myself sound like a dick. "I wasn't sure if I was ready to know."

Asking makes it real. Right now, I can still exist in the space where the tiny shred of doubt lives. Because as much as I'll gladly step up and become Dad of the Year, the idea still terrifies me.

"So you invited her to Christmas instead?"

"Listen, it wasn't my finest moment of thinking on my feet." I meet my brother's scrutinizing gaze. "I told her to bring him with her."

Enzo rolls his eyes. "I know you're brawn and not the brain of this twinship, but not even you can think this is a good idea."

"I don't know," I snap, cutting off anything else he was about to say. "I—Fuck. I don't know."

Unable to sit still, I jump to my feet and round the couch, pacing the length behind it as I try to work through my thoughts. "Leigh is the farthest thing from the person I should be having a child with, but also, I could do worse. And if he is mine, I've already missed so much. I'm angry and confused and have no idea what the hell I'm doing. I just know I needed to do something, and getting them to Telluride under the guise of working on Monarch Hearts seemed like a good idea at the time."

"I get it."

I freeze mid pace and look over my shoulder at him. "Do you?"

"No, not at all." He huffs with a sardonic laugh. "But you know I'm in your corner no matter what. And the guys will be, too, after they get over the fact you invited her to Christmas when you've cock blocked the shit out of them over and over."

"I know," I groan, knowing damn well they are going to make my life hell. Especially Bash.

Fucking Leigh.

I run a frustrated hand through my hair, tugging at the strands at the base of my neck.

How could she not tell me?

I get that we don't exactly have a good history, but we could have fixed things sooner like I wanted to.

But no.

She had to go disappear on me, and then when I had the chance, I fucked it up.

Shit.

We have a kid.

"So what are you going to do?" Enzo's question stops me from continuing on my doom spiral.

"What more can I do?" I ask, a helpless sort of weight anchoring in my chest. "When she gets here, I'm going to ask what the hell she was thinking and demand a paternity test."

"What about Monarch Hearts?"

I scoff. "You and I both know I've had the logistics ironed out for weeks. I spoke with Phillip over at the Lobos Chapter, and he sent over his notes. I'll get the final bit done tomorrow before Leigh gets here. That way, she just needs to sign off on it."

Enzo smirks, reading between the lines. "Was this your plan all along? Get Leigh alone?"

"Before I found out about the kid?" I give him a sheepish shrug. "It's possible. You know I've wanted to fix things for years."

"I know. And after you saw her this past spring, you became obsessive."

Not one of my finer moments. But there is something about that woman that drives me mad. She's fucking incredible. Smart. Sexy. Sarcastic with a side of no bullshit. I know I don't have a chance in hell, but the feral part of me wants to chase her until she lets me keep her.

Of course, I'm not about to tell my twin that. He'll never let me live it down. So I brush him off with a bit of brutish assholery. "She gave quite possibly the best head I've ever had."

"You're disgusting," Enzo huffs with a roll of his eyes, and all I can offer is a half-hearted shrug.

"I never claimed to be otherwise."

He continues to shake his head and faces back toward the crackling fire. "That could be the mother of your child."

"At least I know she's good at it. Especially if she's the only woman I'll be with for the rest of my life," I say as I cross the room and pour us each two fingers of sipping tequila.

"Wait—what?" Enzo whips his head around just as I offer him his glass. "What the hell does that mean?"

He grabs it and clinks it against mine.

"If the kid is mine, I fully intend on marrying that woman."

Enzo manages to avoid spitting out his own tequila, swallowing hard. "Seriously?"

I nod, savoring the delicious flavor with a dash of heat the tequila leaves at the back of my throat.

"You know this isn't the nineteen fifties? You can absolutely have a child and not have to marry someone."

I give a dismissive shrug and sink back onto the couch beside him. "Maybe you could, but not me."

"Where the hell is this coming from?" My brother looks at me like I've grown a second head. "I know you've got some mommy issues, but I never took you for a traditionalist. Not after everything our family put us through."

"Mom and Dad are a cautionary tale, to be sure. Because of them, we were little high society carbon copies of themselves—lie and cheat by whatever means to stay on top. It was toxic, and they stepped out on their marriage repeatedly, but they instilled a sense of family in us."

Enzo snorts into his tequila and takes a sip. "And yet neither of us speaks to them."

I look away to hide my wince, unwilling to let him know about the fifteen missed calls I have from our mother. There's a reason I've been ignoring them.

"True. They may not be the family I choose to surround myself with now, but I appreciate that value. You are my family." I nod to the door that leads to the kitchen, where our best friends are yelling at the football game on the television. "They are my family. I want that for my son. But more than that, I want him to see what I never did—a team when he looks at his parents."

I want that for myself.

Which is why I'm torn when it comes to those missed calls. I can't stop the hope that maybe one day our real family will want the same.

Enzo chews on my words. Literally. I can see his jaw working as he tries to make sense of everything I've just said.

Family isn't something we talk about. Not outside what we have going with Holt and Bash. This is all we need. Or rather, it's all Enzo needs. But me? Lately I feel like I've been searching for something more. Maybe this is it.

Minutes pass until Enzo finally asks, "And you have to be married for that?"

I shrug. "That's just how I always pictured it."

"Damn it, Luca." Enzo drains the last bit of tequila in his glass and lets out a low, frustrated chuckle. "I guess we're doing this. Should I put out an ad in the Los Angeles Times and break hearts everywhere by letting them know Luca Donati is off the market?"

"Get fucked," I joke, finishing off my drink and setting the glass on the coffee table. "Thanks for being in my corner."

"Always." And despite the arrogant smile on his face, I know he means it. "Now you've just got to go out there and tell Bash and Holt your little plan."

I wince as I consider the other two members of our unorthodox family.

Bash is going to love rubbing this in my face. Especially after all the shit I've given him about bringing women back on previous trips. Holt, on the other hand, is going to be a tough sell. Of the four of us, he was the closest to Jack. The most protective of our time together and the sanctity of this trip.

"I was thinking we could just wait until I know if the kid is mine."

Enzo's eyes widen. "You're just going to hide Leigh and the kid in the guest house like a dirty little secret?"

"Okay, so I haven't completely thought this through," I admit.

"Well, it sounds like you have twenty-four hours to figure it out."

Twenty-four hours.

More like torture.

My phone buzzes and I look down to see a nine-oh-six area code.

I don't need a name to know it's my mother.

Hitting the red decline button, I hide the guilt from my face and grin. "Do you get a bachelor party for becoming a dad? Like a last night of freedom."

Enzo rolls his eyes and pushes himself up from the couch. "I don't think that's a thing."

"It should be."

He heads for the door and motions with his hand for me to join him. "How about we go watch the game and you can pretend it's a bachelor party?"

"Nah, I think I'm going to finish up these notes for Monarch Hearts. I've got to convince Leigh to let me put a ring on her finger."

"You're going to have to do more than some paperwork if you ever want that to happen."

"I know." I've already got a ten-point plan formulating in my mind for how I'm going to apologize, win her over, *and* make her pay for keeping this from me in the first place.

All in two days.

It's called balance, right?

"Can you make sure the guys are out of the house tomorrow night around six, so I can sneak Leigh in?"

"Sometimes I hate that you're my twin." Enzo huffs, shaking his head as he pauses at the threshold of the room and looks over his shoulder. "I'll do your dirty work, but for the record, I still think this is a terrible idea."

I offer him a sardonic grin. "Noted."

Once he's gone, I pick up my phone and type Leigh's name into the search bar in the hopes there is a picture of this mystery child somewhere on the Internet. Renegade Hearts is the first thing that pops up, followed by articles covering the incredible things the non-profit is doing. All things I've read at least a hundred times each since spring training at the Orange League Gala.

She was stunning that night. Dressed in a floor-length midnight gown that brought out the blue in her eyes. Glaring at me from across the room as I tried everything in my power to get close to her.

Each time, she managed to slip away.

But not this time.

Chapter Four

LEIGH

The cool winter air hits like a shard of ice, and I pull Zach close, bundling him against me as we exit the private jet Luca sent for us.

Most people wouldn't be happy going from a frozen city to a frozen mountain, but I'm in love.

Inhaling the crisp, clean air, a wave of nostalgia hits me. While these mountains practically kiss the clouds and make the slopes in Michigan look like glorified hills, I can't help but feel a little at home.

I swallow hard, remembering the last time I felt this way, and fight back the tears that come when I think about my parents. Winter was their season and Christmas their holiday. Snowmobiling. Santa. Hot chocolate by the fire. It's been nine years, and it still isn't any easier.

Thank God we will be out of here by the twenty-fifth, so I can smile past the tears for Zach in the privacy of my own home.

"Two days," I whisper. "I can do this."

"Down, Mama," Zach orders, wiggling in my arms.

"Okay," I reluctantly agree, setting him down on the landing outside the plane. "Take my hand and I'll help you with the stairs."

"I do." He looks up at me for permission.

Those big blue eyes of his melt me. Always filled with a hint of wonder and mischief, I'm helpless to do anything but encourage this sweet boy to take on the world ahead of him.

"Okay, you can do it."

I watch with apprehension as Zach reaches for the railing and carefully takes one step at a time, not needing my help.

God, he's getting so big.

Lost in his progress, it's not until he's seventy-five percent of the way down that I look up to see where we are supposed to go after this.

And that's when I see him.

Standing next to a blacked-out SUV, he looks far too hot for it being so damn cold out. Wrapped in a camel-colored trench, paired with black slacks and a button-down that hugs his chest in all the right places, he radiates the wealth of his status. I mean, the guy flew us here on a private jet. It makes sense he wouldn't show up in jeans and a hoodie.

The same cannot be said for me.

Glancing down at my Renegades zip-up and leggings, I realize just how out of my depth I am. The Bennett name might have once been respected in high society, and I might be best friends with a billionaire and an actress, but we are not the same.

Luca pushes off the SUV and starts towards the stairs. He runs his hand through his onyx hair. Cropped short on the sides but tousled on top, it's a look that not many guys can pull off—of course, Luca can.

I force a cordial smile to my lips, but it falls as soon as I realize the glittering blue eyes I love to hate aren't locked on me, but rather on my son.

The significance of the moment bottoms out my stomach. This is it. This could be the first time Zach meets his father.

Maybe.

Then again, maybe not.

Gripping the rail for support, I'm not entirely sure what I'm supposed to do here. I've never been one for sentimental moments, but when it comes to my son, I'm a sucker for them. But there's a part of me that wants to snatch him into my arms and run back up these stairs where the Donatis can't touch us.

But it's not about me.

Not anymore.

Which is why I pull my phone from my jacket pocket, swipe up to the camera app, and snap a picture just as Zach reaches the last step and looks up to where Luca stands in front of him.

"Hey, little man," Luca says, squatting down, so he is eye level with Zach.

Unsolicited tears line my eyes and I blink them away as Zach turns and looks up at me, unsure what to do.

"It's okay," I reassure him. "This is Mommy's friend, Luca. He's going to take us to the hotel we are staying at."

Luca glances up at me, but it's not long enough for me to get a read on him before his eyes are back on Zach. "I've got a surprise for you."

"S'prise?" Zach echoes.

Luca nods. "Do you like baseball?"

Zach tips his little head to the side and smiles. "Cawson?"

I shake my head. Of course, that's who he associates with baseball. Not his godmother. Or even the Renegades in general. It's the guy who uses him as his wingman to pick up women.

Luca tips his head back and laughs, and it's unfair just how beautiful he looks doing so in the light of the setting sun.

"You know Carson?"

Zach nods, enamored with Luca.

"He was on my team once upon a time." He reaches into the pocket of his coat and pulls out a bright purple beanie with glittering gold edges and flaps to cover the ears. Across the front there's a baseball with the word Monarchs stitched in gold underneath. "To keep your ears warm."

Zach reaches up and grabs the hat and looks at it like he's unsure if it's a trap.

If Luca had checked with me, I would have told him hats are not the way to Zach's heart. It doesn't matter how cold it is, or how many little old women have stopped and berated me for allowing him to pull off his beanie, Zach hates having his head covered.

I open my mouth to tell Luca as much, when Zach goes on and makes a liar out of me by tugging on the hat immediately.

Pulling on the strings, he looks up at Luca and beams. "Tanks."

My jaw drops and I pin a murderous glare in Luca's direction. Thankfully, he's still ignoring me. I don't have to explain why I'm ready to yank that damn hat away and pretend the last five minutes never happened.

I know I'm overreacting.

I know it's not a slight against me.

Zach just likes the hat.

At least he remembered his manners.

But then why does it feel like Luca just won for Dad of the Year when he's known the kid all of ten seconds?

"You're welcome," Luca says, his eyes still locked on my son, not understanding the huge feat he's just accomplished as he continues to ignore me. "You ready to go, bud?"

"Go!" Zach repeats loudly, clutching his stuffed horse to his chest with one hand and reaching out to offer Luca his other hand.

Why couldn't I have had a kid with crippling stranger danger? No, instead he takes to people like a fish to water and strives to be everyone's best friend.

Without looking back, Luca and Zach walk hand in hand to the SUV. As I follow behind, my heart constricts in my chest, and I fight the feeling that I'm losing my son.

It's irrational, but that doesn't stop it from sticking to the forefront of my brain like dog hair on a black shirt.

Maybe this was a mistake.

Luca and Zach reach the car, and I realize his car seat is still on the plane.

"Wait, we need to grab his car seat," I call out as Luca opens the back door.

Without acknowledging me, Luca picks Zach up and places him in the car. "I already had one installed."

"Oh," I mumble, and I'm not sure if I should be impressed or irritated by his forethought with only twenty-four hours' notice.

Definitely impressed, right?

He buckles Zach in, which I double check to make sure is tight enough and the straps are in the right place.

Of course they are. And here I was worried about him not putting in the effort. Instead, he's ten steps ahead of me and ready to take my place.

If he is Zach's dad, would he really do that?

Would he take him from me?

No. Right?

My breath seizes and I grip the car door for support as I close my eyes and try to calm my racing heart.

Breathe in.

And out.

Zach will always be my son. He's not going anywhere.

I open my eyes and see the smiling face of the little boy that is my world.

"Go, Momma."

His sweet little voice is enough to ground me.

Leaning in, I press a kiss to his forehead. "Yup, we're gonna go."

After double checking the buckles one more time, I shut the door behind me and turn to climb in the front seat but instead I'm greeted with Luca's chest against my cheek.

Air knocked from my lungs, I stumble back. Luca's hand darts out and wraps around my waist, stopping me from hitting the ground.

"Thanks," I rasp.

When he doesn't respond, I make the mistake of glancing up. Any hope of seeing the man who impressed my best friends and helped save the Renegades disappears. Gone is the glittering smile and twinkling eyes reserved for my son, replaced by darkness as cold as the wind whipping through the trees.

This is the Luca Donati I remember. Cold. Calculating. And overall a grade A dick.

"You should have told me," he snaps, his voice devoid of any joy.

Yanking my arm from his grip, I step back and narrow my gaze and channel diplomacy despite my heart being in my throat. "This isn't how I wanted you to find out."

His lip curls into a sneer. "No, you didn't want me to find out at all."

"Luca, that's not—"

"We'll talk about this later," he bites, his eyes darting to the dark glass that separates my son from us. "We don't need Zach hearing us argue."

It's on the tip of my tongue to inform him I'm perfectly capable of outlining all the reasons he's being a jackass without my son knowing a damn thing—since he's a toddler and doesn't understand half of what we say—but instead, I bite my lower lip and stop myself.

If he wants to wait to talk, I'm not going to twist his arm. Especially when he's right. I didn't want him to know about Zach.

Luca turns on his heel and rounds the front of the SUV, leaving me standing there cold, angry, and confused as I try my best to recover from the emotional whiplash of my first ten minutes in Colorado.

My tired reflection greets me in the mirrored glass of the window as I turn to open the door. "Buck up, buttercup," I whisper to myself as if it's somehow going to help. "It's going to be a long ass few days."

Chapter Five

WILLOW: When were you going to tell us you are going on a mountain holiday with Luca?

INDIE: She's doing what now?

WILLOW: LEIGHTON RENEE BENNETT.

INDIE: oh shit. She full full named you.

WILLOW: Why is Luca asking me what Zach's favorite foods are and if he's in a forward or rear facing car seat?

INDIE: What is happening?

WILLOW: Apparently our sweet little Leigh let the cat out of the bag and now her baby daddy is whisking her and Zach off to Telluride for the weekend.

INDIE: I want a baby daddy to whisk me off somewhere romantic.

WILLOW: We both know you don't want to be tied down to just one dick, and you hate kids.

INDIE: I don't hate Zach. And I love Bishop's goddaughter. What's her name?

WILLOW: Phoebe

INDIE: Yeah. I love Zach and Phoebe.

WILLOW: And both of them love you. But still, no baby daddies. We can only deal with one at a time.

INDIE: Agreed. Plus, kids are sticky.

WILLOW: That's your objection?

INDIE: I'm a simple woman.

WILLOW: Leigh you better call us the minute you touch down in Telluride.

LEIGH: I thought I'd have a whole two days free from those stupid dancing trolls. So would you like to clue me in as to why they're the first thing Luca turned on in the car, claiming they're Zach's favorites?

LEIGH: You wouldn't happen to know anything about that would you Willow?

WILLOW: Shit. That's my fault. I told him that if Zach had meltdowns they were the only thing that would calm him. I thought I was helping.

LEIGH: I know you did but from now on please just let me handle this.

WILLOW: So you told him about Zach.

LEIGH: Unintentionally.

INDIE: Is he still as hot as I remember?

LEIGH: Hotter.

INDIE: Does he have that whole dad vibe going on?

LEIGH: Let's not get ahead of ourselves. He might not be the father.

WILLOW: But I mean he gets points for trying to make sure he has everything he needs for Zach there.

LEIGH: He does. But that doesn't make up for being an asshole the minute Zach isn't looking.

INDIE: HE DID WHAT?

WILLOW: <face palm emoji> Damn it, Luca.

LEIGH: We are just pulling up to the house. I'll call you when I get settled.

INDIE: That sounds so domestic. Is Luca going to cook you dinner and tuck you in too?

LEIGH: <sinking face emoji> We ate on the plane. And I'm not staying with Luca. Well not really.

WILLOW: It sounds like there's a story there.

LEIGH: There is.

LEIGH: Apparently wanting my own accommodation means staying in the guest house of their vacation home.

INDIE: oh now that's romantic.

WILLOW: Maybe you should just enjoy the vacation. I mean obviously also get the Monarch Hearts thing done. But also, vacation.

LEIGH: Don't encourage this.

INDIE: Never. Why would we do that? It's not like you're a workaholic and need a break.

INDIE: Or you know, a wild night in bed.

LEIGH: How many times do I have to tell you that's not going to happen?

INDIE: TWO YEARS LEIGHTON!

INDIE: Your pussy probably has cobwebs he'll need to dust away.

LEIGH: <middle finger emoji> I like the family of spiders that's taken up residence.

LEIGH: If I need to come, I'll just use the pocket vibrator you got me last Christmas.

INDIE: You brought Frenchy with you?

LEIGH: Always. That little fry has never done me wrong.

WILLOW: I still can't believe you got her that so in case it fell out of her purse she could just say Zach dropped a French fry in her purse.

INDIE: It was a genius idea. That little fry has ten settings all guaranteed to make you see stars. Right, Leigh?

LEIGH: And on that note, I am going inside.

LEIGH: Willow, no more helping the enemy.

WILLOW: Fine. But if he asks your favorite position, I'm going to tell him.

LEIGH: <eye roll emoji> I regret annotating those books so thoroughly.

INDIE: You love us and don't you dare stop. The sisterhood of the traveling smut will never recover if you do.

Chapter Six

LUCA

How is it possible for a human so little to have such excruciating screams?

It's a miracle Leigh can still hear after being in such proximity to the tiny banshee.

I bundle myself deeper into my coat and step closer to the bonfire pit to keep warm. But mostly to stop myself from crossing the deck and demanding Leigh let me into the guesthouse.

Not that I would know what the hell to do, because I absolutely don't. The last time I was around a toddler was when my sister *was* the toddler. Seeing as I'm only four-and-a-half years older than her, the most I did was hand her a toy to soothe her.

Still, I don't understand how Leigh can stand listening to him cry like this.

It's heartbreaking.

Then again, he's been fighting against her request to go to bed for the last forty-five minutes, so maybe we are approaching it being a tad dramatic.

I'm just grateful Holt insisted on renting out the entire property, including the guesthouse, even though we didn't plan to use the additional rooms. I can't even imagine having to explain to someone that we're not trying to kill this kid. He just doesn't want to go to bed. As it is, I have no idea how I'm going to hide them from the guys for the next two days. But that's a problem for future Luca because I have to admit, I like the idea of having Zach close by.

Leigh, on the other hand, was not thrilled with the proximity.

Zach lets out another wail and my chest constricts, wishing I could stop his cries.

Is this what it's like to become a parent? Is this that instantaneous love the guys who have kids on the team were always talking about?

I think back to his sweet toothy smile and messy hair the same shade of white blonde as his mother's. His blue eyes that, if not for the white hue that line his irises would be identical to mine.

I've always wanted kids—eventually—but I never considered who'd they'd be or what they'd look like. I never wondered if they'd like baseball or have a penchant for piano like my brother. I've never asked myself if I'd be a good dad.

One look at that little boy and I'm considering every single one of those things and so much more.

While Zach brought out this whimsical paternal side of me, seeing Leigh made me want to rage in a way I hadn't expected. It took everything in me not to go off on her on the tarmac.

She's the reason I missed his entrance into the world.

The reason I never heard his first words or witnessed his first steps.

And yet she's still the most beautiful fucking woman I've ever laid eyes on.

It's unfair the way I'd like nothing more than to take her over my knee and spank her for her sins. Only to follow it up with getting on my knees for her and begging her to forgive me for mine. Followed by a desperate plea to allow me to be a part of my son's life.

Talk about emotional whiplash.

My brain is a scary place to be at the moment.

Another twenty minutes pass before quiet takes over the guesthouse.

Even though I'm fairly certain my toes are numb and on the verge
of frostbite, I wait another ten before I pick up my peace offering of
expensive wine and tequila and cross the deck.

The bottles clink together as I struggle to hold them in one hand and
lift the other to knock.

Once.

Twice.

The door whips open, and Leigh is there before my knuckles hit a
third time. "What the fuck are you th—"

She doesn't get to finish her statement when, from the back of the
guesthouse, Zach lets out an endless wail.

"Fucking damn it." Leigh's shoulders sag in defeat, and I immediately
feel like shit.

"Oh, fuck," I mutter in panic. "I'm sorry. I didn't think—"

"Of course you didn't," Leigh cuts me off, her eyes darting from me
to the direction of Zach's room.

"What the hell does that mean?" I counter. Hackles instantly raised
despite the fact they help exactly no one in this situation.

Leigh rolls her big blue eyes and sighs. "Nothing. What are you even
doing here? Because if it's not an emergency, I'm kinda busy."

God, I'm fucking this up. I didn't come over here to fight.

Or maybe I did.

But I didn't mean to make things worse.

Pushing down my pride, I ask, "How can I help?"

"You've done enough." Her rejection is a slap to the face, but at least
she doesn't slam the door in it. Instead, she turns on her heel and heads to
the back of the small apartment.

The thought of leaving doesn't even cross my mind.

Setting the bottles on the small kitchen island, I follow Leigh down
the hallway, past the main bedroom and to the smaller room that doubles

as a guest room and office space.

The glow from the Christmas lights I strung around the window illuminates enough of the room that I can see her approach the daybed. She sits on top of what looks like a large pile of pillows tucked under the sheet, making a wall between the edge and where Zach lays. Leigh's voice softens as she coaxes the overtired two-year-old to lie down and go back to sleep.

Zach, of course, has other plans.

Struggling to keep his eyes open, he shoots up and wraps his tiny arms around his mom's waist.

"Tay," Zach whimpers against her, and Leigh immediately begins to rub her hand up and down his back to soothe him.

At this point, I'd like to say I'm keeping it together, but I'm seconds away from losing it. This simple act of a mother tending to her son is like watching a movie in a foreign language. My mother would never have shown us that kind of tenderness. My siblings and I had nannies and each other.

This is—it's everything.

"I'm just across the hall, my sweet boy," Leigh reassures him. "And I can see you just like I can at home." She points to the small camera on top of the bedside table she must have brought with her.

Zach's sleepy gaze tracks across the bed and back up to Leigh. "Sea."

She heaves a sigh—one even I can see is filled with nothing but love—and leans down and presses a kiss to his forehead. "Okay. Last time though."

"Sea," Zach repeats as he lies back and snuggles down into the comforter. He clings to the stuffed horse he arrived with, and I get the feeling he's never without.

Leaning against the doorframe like a damn voyeur, I watch as Leigh's shoulders rise with an inhale, and when they fall, she begins to sing.

My jaw drops, and if I wasn't already adhering to a vow of silence in order to not wake Zach again, I'd be too stunned to make a sound.

The lullaby isn't a happy one, only made more hauntingly beautiful by the woman who takes each word and gives it life. I swear I've heard it somewhere before, though I'm not sure where. It's about a mother singing to her daughter, telling her to go where the wind meets the sea—to follow the truth but not lose sight of who you are and drown.

There is no way it's a kid's bedtime song. At the same time, I completely understand why Zach likes it. Especially when it's Leigh singing like she is right now. It's almost ethereal. Which is not a word I would ever use to describe the blonde spitfire. But this vulnerable side she saves for her son—this side of her I didn't know existed—it's magic.

Lost in my thoughts, I don't notice the room go silent or Leigh move to stand in front of me. It's only when she grunts that I look up and find her soft and loving gaze has been replaced with daggers.

"Out. Now," she rasps low enough there's barely any sound.

And just like that, we're back to the inevitable fight brewing between us. It needs to happen, but now that I've seen her with Zach, I'm not sure I want to.

I just want to be on the same page.

Sliding out of the doorway, I gesture for her to lead the way and follow silently behind.

When she reaches the kitchen, she grabs the bottle of tequila and points a finger at the couch in the attached living room. "Sit. Now."

"Do you want me to get you a glass?"

"Oh no, the time for glasses and polite conversation has passed." There's fire in her gaze as she twists off the cap and brings the bottle to her lips…and takes two long pulls of what is absolutely not shooting tequila—not that I'm about to correct her. "Right now, you're going to get your ass outside, and we are going to get a few things straight."

It might be the point-blank order, or maybe it's the fire in her gaze paired with the knowledge that—despite her hating me—I know what it sounds like hearing her cry my name when she comes. Either way, I'm pretty sure there's no world in which this situation should make my dick twitch. Yet here I am, ready to mutter an emphatic *yes, ma'am* and do whatever she says.

"It's forty-one degrees outside," I remind her softly, not wanting to talk back, but also my toes are only just getting feeling back in them.

"And?"

"Even by the fire, it's fucking cold."

Leigh huffs a sardonic laugh. "Well, you should have thought of that before you came barging in here, waking up my over tired, out of sorts toddler. Who, I might add, wouldn't even be out of sorts if it wasn't for your insistence that I had to come *here* to do my job."

Is she fucking kidding me?

If I wasn't ready to fight, I am now.

"It seems to me you are forgetting some key details in that recap, don't you think? How about the part where you never told me about the fact we made a fucking child together, so that's why I had to do whatever it took to get you here?"

Okay, so that might be stretching the truth a little, but I don't give a shit. I am not the only one at fault here.

I eat the space between us in two long strides until I'm only inches in front of her. She cranes her neck to meet my gaze, and I zero in on the small vein bulging just above her left eye.

"Outside," she demands through a clenched jaw.

"No."

Her chest brushes against mine as her breath hitches, her voice straining to keep it together. "Luca, I swear to God, I will kill you if that little boy wakes up again. So if you want to keep your body void of any kitchen knives, I suggest you get your savory, little Italian ass outside."

God, she's delicious when she's riled up.

I arch a brow. "My ass is savory?"

Never did I imagine her being an ass kind of woman, but I'll save that away for later.

"Out," she growls.

Picking up the bottle of tequila, as I'm sure she'll appreciate the liquid sweater when she realizes just how cold it is, I head for the door with Leigh hot on my heels. She grabs her hoodie from the hook and silently slides into the chair on the opposite side of the firepit.

The fire dances between us, its crackle the only sound before Leigh heaves a great sigh, losing some of her fight. "We can't argue like that in front of Zach."

"Agreed." I nod.

"He doesn't like it when people yell."

Immediately, I'm on the defensive. "Did something happen?"

Who do I need to kill?

Leigh rolls her eyes. "No, he's almost two. He's afraid of his own shadow. Yelling just scares him."

My brow furrows as I recall our conversation the day before and how old she said Zach was. "Almost two? I thought he was two."

Leigh stands up and rounds the firepit, grabbing the bottle of tequila from the table beside me. She takes another long pull and heads back to her chair, bottle in hand. "His birthday is January 1st. It's just easier to say two since we're so close."

Yet another thing I didn't know about him.

Is this how it's always going to feel? Like I'm late to the game, trying to figure out the rules and regulations while having one hand tied behind my back. My fists clench in my lap, and the anger that has ebbed and flowed since I learned about Zach rears its ugly head.

"Anything else I should know about my son?"

"No." Leigh doesn't hesitate. Which only serves to annoy me further.

"Is it terrible I find that hard to believe?" I seethe, teetering between wanting to fight with her and pleading for her to understand where I'm coming from.

Her eyes glitter through the fire. Fierce. Steeled. Resolved. "I'm only doing what's best for Zach."

"And that's shutting me out?" I snap, my voice dancing a line of irate and desperate.

"For now? Maybe."

"What the hell does that mean?" My nostrils flare as my grasp on the conversation slips further and further away from me.

This isn't how this is supposed to go. I knew we'd have our issues. I knew I'd have to grovel a bit to fix what I broke all those years ago. But I never expected she'd admit point-blank to wanting to keep me from my son.

And yet I understand it.

I hate it.

But I understand it.

She doesn't know me. Not anymore. Not that she really did. She only ever saw what my mother wanted her to see. Because that's how it was growing up a Donati.

"Fuck," I curse under my breath as I run my hand through my hair, my gaze lost in the fire.

"You're not the only guy I slept with that week." Her words are little more than a shy whisper, but they carry the weight of a sledgehammer, garnering my full attention.

Time stops as I work out what she's implying.

That means—

I might not be—

But his eyes.

They're my eyes.

My heart seizes in my chest as it shatters for the life I've been building in my head for the last twenty-four hours.

Fuck.

I did it again.

Got ahead of myself—jumped in head first without all the facts.

But it's never backfired like this. Somehow, everything always ends up working out.

It never felt like a dream was being ripped away.

I'm Luca fucking Donati.

I make things happen.

I don't fail.

Which only goes to show how badly I wanted this to be a reality.

Lifting my gaze from the fiery logs, I'm greeted with Leigh's pitying stare.

My voice is strained when I finally find it. "So he's not mine?"

"There's—" She fumbles over the words. "There's a possibility Zach isn't your son."

"Your son?" Two shocked voices echo Leigh's words, and I curse at the universe's version of karmic retribution.

Fuck. I don't need this right now.

Leigh and I both turn toward the voices, but I don't need to look to know that the night just got more complicated for me.

Standing at the entrance to the deck from the driveway are my brother, Holt, and Bash—the latter two with their jaws hanging wide open.

"Your timing is impeccable," I grit out, eyes locked on my twin.

Enzo shrugs. "You knew we'd be back when the day slope session was over. It's not my fault you chose to keep her outside instead of hidden away like you promised."

Fucking hell.

Leigh whips her head back to me. "Hidden away?"

A shit-eating grin creeps across Enzo's face. Clearly, he knew his choice of words would no doubt cause problems.

I shoot him a death glare as if to say, *what the fuck, you're supposed to be my twin. That means you're on my side.*

He just shrugs.

I will so fucking remember this moment the next time he needs me to cover for him.

"Will someone tell me what is going on and who the hell this is?" Bash asks as he opens the waist-height gate and crosses the deck, haphazardly tossing his snowboard to the floor. Enzo and Holt follow closely behind and do the same.

"Leigh James," Leigh says as she stands and takes an uneasy step away from the two assholes coming in hot with scowls on their faces.

They both give her a cursory glance before returning their wrath to me.

"What the fuck is this about?" Holt demands.

I expected them to freak out, but that's got nothing on the hurt etched across their faces. I'm two for two on fucking up today.

"I'm—I'm sorry to crash your vacation," Leigh stammers, trying to defuse the situation. "Luca's doing me a favor, since we have to get some work done before the end of the year."

"Seriously?" Bash snaps at the same time Holt yells, "What the fuck, Luca? Work and pussy? You know the rules."

Leigh glances at me, a brow raised. "I take it you didn't tell them."

"They weren't supposed to see you," I grumbled before turning to my friends. "I'll explain everything inside."

Leigh lifts a hand and presses her lips together. "No need. I should be getting inside to make sure Zach's still asleep. I'll see about getting out of your hair tomorrow, guys."

"Oh no, little thief," I say, closing the distance between us and wrapping a hand around her bicep. "We aren't finished yet."

"I think we are." She looks down at my hand and back up at me. "You only call me that when you're angry."

"And think I have every right to be."

"Honestly, you can stay, Leigh," Bash purrs. "Luca is the one who can find his way home."

"I should go." Leigh pulls her hand from the pocket of her hoodie, wraps her dainty fingers around mine, and loosens them from her arm. "We can talk in the morning."

I should say yes and let her walk away.

But of course, when it comes to this woman, I can't help but pour gasoline on the raging fire between us.

"I want a paternity test." The words roll off my tongue more harshly than I intend, but the desired effect is there.

Bottom line, I'm an asshole, but I'm an asshole who doesn't like to lose.

Leigh's shoulders deflate, but it doesn't feel as good as I thought it might. She nods as she reaches into her pocket and pulls out a clear plastic bag that I didn't know she had, a glimmer of sadness in her eyes. "I figured you would."

Stretching out her hand, she offers it to me. Inside are two swabs, each in individual test tubes and a second one that is sealed. "This already has Zach's DNA. You just need to swab your cheek and stick it in the mail."

My lips part in shock but quickly twist in a sneer. "You think I'm going to trust that you actually swabbed his cheek and didn't just give me yours, so you could keep him from me?"

Leigh winces.

God, I just keep digging this hole, but I can't stop myself. It's like an accident—and I'm watching myself crash and burn because I can't see past my own anger.

At myself for believing I could have the family I've always wanted.

At Enzo for not doing his damn job and keeping the guys away.

Again, at myself, for thinking this was a good idea in the first place.

At Leigh for keeping all these fucking secrets from me.

"I deserve that," she agrees, "which is why the second one in there is mine. They can test it and prove he's my son, and then yours will be the wildcard."

My eyes lock on the test in my hand, and I stand there, dumbfounded—unsure of how to deal with the ache in my chest or the guilt in my soul.

God, this is a clusterfuck.

When I finally look up, Leigh is already halfway across the deck, muttering another round of "sorry" to Bash, Holt, and Enzo as she makes her way to the guesthouse.

My eyes stay glued to her until the door is securely closed.

"You have some serious fucking explaining to do," Bash grunts, grabbing the bottle of tequila Leigh left behind.

Holt crosses the path and bumps my shoulder with his fist as he makes his way to one of the free chairs by the fire. "Yeah, what happened to bros before hoes?"

"Watch your fucking mouth," I snap. Leigh might be the sniper holding the rifle zeroed in on my life, but she's still possibly the mother of my child.

"No, but seriously." Bash takes a long pull from the bottle. "Does this mean I can bring home the sweet little German girl from the slopes? Or do I have to have a baby with her for that privilege?"

His sarcasm lifts a slight weight from my chest. Bash's joking means we'll be okay. Not that he's going to let me off easily, but it tells me he'll at least hear me out. Holt will follow suit.

My brother offers a wicked I-told-you-so grin. "On that note, I'll grab another bottle of tequila."

Cheeky bastard.

Chapter Seven

LEIGH

The pre-dawn light filters through the tiny guest house and bounces off the too cheery Christmas decorations I'm assuming Luca added around the guesthouse.

If he wasn't such an asshole, it might be sweet.

I peer into the spare bedroom where Zach is still sleeping soundly, squeezing his stuffed horse.

My heart flutters in the way it can only do now that I'm a mother. It's a blessing and a curse, really. With it comes the realization that he's growing into an amazing kid, but also that each day is one closer to him being grown up. I never understood what my mother meant when she used to tell me I'd always be her baby.

Now I do.

He'll always be the little boy who made me a mom.

But now I might have to share him.

With Luca, of all people.

My brow furrows and anxiety replaces the flutter in my chest as I replay his reaction to finding out Zach might not be his last night.

The whole night could've gone better.

It also could've gone worse.

So much worse.

I'd be lying if I said Luca's anger didn't catch me off guard. I thought he'd be happy to find out there's a possibility he could keep his bachelor lifestyle. He's the face of Donati Brothers Investments and Monarchs baseball. Every day is a game or grand opening of a new property or club. None of which is conducive to being a family man.

My thoughts drift to Willow's dad. He lived for the Renegades, and his daughter paid the price. Not that she didn't love going to the field, but it wasn't exactly the family dynamic she dreamed of.

It's not what I had growing up. A home filled with two loving parents who would do anything and everything to make me smile. I was the center of their world, just like Zach is mine.

The ache that returns every time I think of my parents slithers through me. Tears prick the corner of my eyes, and I swallow hard past the lump of emotion in my throat.

I really freaking miss them.

They would know what to do here.

My mom would tell me family is the most important thing, and my dad would remind me to listen to my mom.

They would have loved Zach.

And probably still hate Luca for everything he did to me.

But they would put Zach first.

Always.

Losing the battle against my tears, a single drop rolls down my cheek.

Damn it.

I want to use last night as a reason to head back to New York this morning, but now that I've laid on the dead-parental-guilt thick, there's no way I'm leaving without at least trying to make amends with the asshole who may or may not be my son's father.

Trying being the operative word.

And I'm definitely not going to enjoy it, that's for damn sure.

But first—before anything—coffee.

Twenty minutes of searching later, it's apparent that Luca was wholly prepared for the arrival of my son. However, it's also clear my best friends didn't warn him of what an absolute terror I'll become if I don't get my morning cup of coffee—or three.

Pulling out my phone, I swipe to the baby monitor app, so I can keep an eye on Zach while in search of the second love of my life.

The sun warms my face despite the frigid morning temps as I exit the guesthouse and cross the small deck to the main house—if it can even be called that. Mansion is more like it.

On the outskirts of the main town of Telluride, the three-story house backs up against the mountain and allows for easy access to the slopes. Which answers how the guys showed up last night without Luca or me hearing them.

I test the side door and exhale a sigh of relief when I find it's unlocked. It swings open into a mudroom equipped with lockers for ski equipment, along with a sink and wash bay, but that's not what snags my attention the most.

It's the heady aroma of my favorite breakfast beverage, making my mouth water. My nose knows a French dark roast when I smell it, and I'm helpless to do anything but follow the direction it's coming from.

Exiting the mudroom, I find myself in a kitchen bigger than my entire New York apartment. Cupboards line one wall, separated by a full range and industrial-size refrigerator. Along the opposite wall, floor-to-ceiling windows offer breathtaking views of the mountainside. That view—coupled with the light color scheme of the kitchen—gives an airy feel to the space. It's everything I would want in a kitchen. Including the ginormous island that splits the room, housing six barstools and, most importantly, a small wine fridge.

And every inch of it is covered in some type of garland or holiday decor.

"Wow," I whisper. These guys don't fuck around when it comes to Christmas.

"This is nothing. You should see the house we stayed at in Belize. Now that was luxury."

Startled, I spin toward the disembodied voice that I'm pretty sure came from behind the cabinets.

"Um, hello?" I ask, taking a few more steps into the kitchen.

Just as I do, a head pops out of what I can now see is a galley style pantry behind the wall of cupboards. It's the guy who came storming onto the deck last night, demanding to know who the hell I was. His medium brown skin has a bronze glow to it that makes me wonder if he's also from California. God knows we aren't getting that much sun in New York this time of year. Wet, curly black hair is plastered to his forehead from a shower or a workout, and the smile he's got on his face is far too big for the sun only just coming up.

Then again, at least he's in a better mood than he was last night.

"I'm guessing you're here for coffee?" he asks, and I try to place his accent. It's a mix between British and Australian—not too proper, but not quite laid back.

"Is there any other way to start the morning?" I counter as he disappears back into the pantry.

Navigating around the island, I follow him inside and my jaw drops at the sheer size. It's practically a second kitchen with every appliance imaginable and fully stocked shelves.

Clearly unaffected by the pantry of my dreams, Luca's friend continues as he pours each of us a mug.

"No, coffee is the nectar of the gods, but I'm the only one of the four of us that drinks the stuff. Enzo is snooty with his tea, and Luca becomes a damn energizer bunny if you give him even a drop of caffeine." He kneels and pulls a carafe out of a hidden fridge in the cabinet below. "Cream?"

"Yes, please." He steps back and allows me to pour a splash into the dark roast. "So Enzo likes tea and we need to avoid giving Luca coffee—that accounts for three of you."

"Holt prefers some mushroom blend that he swears is the same as coffee, but really, he's full of shit and it tastes like dirt."

I scrunch my nose. "Who would disrespect coffee that way?"

"Exactly."

The eyes of my coffee cohort watch me as I slip the carafe back in the fridge. It's a bit unnerving, but I get it. I'm the girl who crashed their apparently sacred Christmas.

Rising to my full height, albeit way shorter than him, I lift my narrowed gaze to meet his caramel eyes. "So that accounts for three of the four. Which would make you?"

"Sebastian Hart." He extends a hand, and when I place mine in his, he grips it firmly.

"It's nice to meet you, Sebastian."

He huffs a laugh and brings my hand to lips, pressing a light kiss to my knuckles. "You can call me Bash. Especially If I'm about to be an uncle to your kid."

So he's the shameless flirt of the group.

Noted.

I raise a skeptical brow. "And who says you are?"

"You're the baby momma, right?"

"Ha," I scoff. He makes it sound so simple. "Maybe. Maybe not."

Bash winks and, paired with the accent, I'm sure it's a tactic to win over hearts and panties everywhere.

Too bad I'm immune to the bullshit of athletes.

Well, most of them anyway.

"Then I'm definitely Bash." His smile falters. "Unless the kid's not Luca's. Then I guess we'll have to see if he keeps you around."

"What if I don't keep him around?" I counter.

"Eh." Bash shrugs and turns on his heel, heading back to the kitchen. "I wouldn't blame you."

My eyes go wide. He wouldn't?

"Aren't you supposed to be on his side?" What kind of friends does Luca have that they would side with a woman they just met? One he is clearly not a fan of at the moment.

"Oh, I am. But as his friend, I also know Luca is a special brand of extra. He jumps without looking and fumbles for his parachute on the way down."

That is one hundred percent not how I would describe the Luca I remember. He was a minion of his parents—wealthy, calculating and self-serving. He didn't do anything without an agenda.

Bash extends a hand toward the stool next to him, gesturing for me to join. "Plus, I really should be thanking you."

"Thanking me?" I reluctantly lower myself onto the barstool, leaving one between us. I pull out my phone and prop it up on the lazy Susan in front of me in case Zach wakes up.

Bash leans over and looks before settling back into his chair, arms crossed over his chest. "Absolutely, with you here, this means I can convince Luca to relax his rules of no woman at Bucket List Christmas."

Laughter bubbles from me. It's such a typical guy answer. And yet there's a part of my heart—one I loathe to admit exists—that melts just a tiny bit at the thought that Luca is the one who protects this time with his friends. It's something I understand. He's the Indie of their group. Relating him to my own friend group almost makes him seem a bit more human. Which is not something I thought I'd equate to Luca.

Shit.

Does this mean I have to admit to Willow she might be right about him?

Might.

"Don't hurt yourself thinking, Baby Momma."

Bash pulls me from my thoughts, and I look up to see him sipping his coffee. "I'm never gonna ditch that nickname, am I?"

He grins. "Probably not."

"Great." Frowning, I take a sip from the steaming mug in front of me.

It's just the pick me up I need because the moment the coffee hits my lips, it takes everything in me to stifle a satisfying moan. This coffee is bold and sweet with a hint of spice, and I'm not sure where it came from, but I need to find out if I can get it in New York.

"So, what's Bucket List Christmas?" I lean forward and plant my elbows on the island on either side of my coffee, resting my steepled fingers in front of my chin. "And why do you want to bring women?"

Bash's eyebrows shoot up. "Luca didn't tell you what you were walking in on?"

I chuckle. "It seems he has a habit of keeping secrets."

"Then again, so do you." His smirk says he's playing, but also that he's not afraid to call me on my bullshit.

"Well, you just say it how it is." It's refreshing, and I decide here and now I like this guy.

Bash shrugs and brings his mug to his lips. "Life's too short not to."

"Is this the part where you tell me that if I lie again and break his heart, you'll break my face?"

"A pretty face like yours? No." He tilts his head to the side dramatically, like he's thinking far too hard for this early in the morning. "Though I can't promise Holt won't. He's got a penchant for collecting teeth."

My eyes bulge, and I nearly choke on the coffee I was attempting to swallow. "What?"

"He's a hockey player," Bash clarifies.

"Ahh." I nod, making the connection. "For who?"

"He doesn't play anymore. Nasty knee injury. Now he owns the San Diego Tide."

"Wow, three team owners in one friend group."

"Four," Bash quips.

"Four?"

Bash takes another sip, then smiles and stands. Doing his best Vanna White impersonation, he swipes a hand across his chest, highlighting the team's name under a large growling bear. "Four owners. The San Francisco Grizzlies are owned by yours truly."

"So let me get this straight. You're all team owners, and you celebrate Christmas together." Who are these men, and how the hell did I get here with them? This is like something straight out of a Hallmark movie.

"Something like that."

An amused cackle escapes me. "And I thought being friends with a bunch of Major League ballplayers was surreal."

"So." Bash sits down and leans forward, resting his elbows on the island with his head turned toward me. "Why are you really here, Leigh? Because I'm not buying this bullshit story that you're here just for work."

I look away, my stomach churning. What am I supposed to say?

The simple answer is my guilty conscience. Both in regards to Luca and the fact I don't want to fail Willow and Renegade Hearts.

The complicated answer is—well, just that…complicated.

Not that I expect Bash to understand or even agree, but that's all I got. So that's what I go with.

"Initially, that's exactly why I agreed to come. But also, I think there's a part of me that wanted Luca to know about Zach. Even if he might not be his father. If he is, Zach deserves a dad."

It's more than I planned to reveal to one of Luca's friends, but the moment the words leave my mouth, a small weight lifts off my chest. Maybe Bash is right—life's too short not to say it how it is.

Bash presses his lips together thoughtfully. "You really don't know who his dad is?"

It's the million-dollar question that shouldn't make me feel like shit, but does.

My eyes fall to the countertop. "No."

No one has point blank called me a slut for sleeping with two guys so close together—least of all me—but that doesn't mean I judge myself for it. That week was completely out of the ordinary for me. Historically, I'm a one-man-at-a-time kind of gal. It's hard enough fitting one person in my schedule while running Renegade Hearts, let alone two. The other guy—I think his name was Tod. Maybe Tony. I don't know. He was a victim of my once a year hook up with a random guy because I get a little twitchy and destructive around the anniversary of my parents' death.

And Luca…well, he wasn't part of the plan in any way, shape, or form. He just happened to be there during that moment of weakness with a hate fuck proposition I couldn't pass up.

I'm not proud of myself, but I can't be mad either.

That week gave me Zach.

Thirty seconds pass, and I brace for Bash to call me out. Fully ready to defend myself. But he doesn't. Instead, with a soft, almost tender voice, he asks, "And if Luca is his dad?"

As much as I want to keep my eyes trained on the tiny flecks of gold on the marble countertop and ignore his question, I force myself to meet Bash's. "It feels wrong having this conversation with you and not him."

The right corner of his mouth twitches up, and he chuckles. "With as angry as he was last night, maybe it's better you have it with me first."

I consider his words. I'm stuck here at least until I can get the proposal for Monarch Hearts signed off on. And if Luca is Zach's dad,

I'd really like to be at least friendly co-parents with him. Plus, Bash is easy to talk to. And he's given me a hell of a lot more insight into the man who might be the father of my child than I had when I arrived here.

"Well," I sigh. "In that case, the honest answer is, it's complicated."

"How so?"

"Luca and I—We aren't just strangers who hooked up and made a kid." Though it would be so much easier if we were. "We have a history. And not a good one. He made my life miserable when I was a teenager."

"He *was* a bit of a prick before we got ahold of him." Bash laughs and finishes off the last bit of his coffee. "You hungry?"

As if it knew the question asked, my stomach rumbles. "Starving apparently."

Bash claps his hands down on the island and smiles as he pushes himself up. "Good. Breakfast is my specialty. Does Zach like pancakes?"

"Loves them." I smile, touched he'd consider my son.

"Perfect."

I silently watch as Bash makes his way back into the pantry and comes out with his hands filled with everything needed to feed an army instead of five adults and a toddler.

"Do you need any help?" I ask, the manners my mother instilled in me shining through.

Bash drops everything on the island, the flour bag puffing out a giant white cloud. "I'm more of a solo man in the kitchen. But you can sit there and keep lookin' gorgeous."

I find myself rolling my eyes again. Something, it seems, that's impossible to avoid when chatting with Bash. Finishing off my coffee, I help myself to another. When I return to my seat at the island, Bash is humming to himself as he whips the batter together in a large bowl.

He reminds me a lot of the guys on the Renegades—grown ass adults, thriving at what they do, yet managing to somehow teeter the line of cocky and down to earth.

My dad used to say, *you are the people you surround yourself with*. Maybe that's why I was drawn to Willow and Indie. I was the new kid who just wanted to be included, and they took me in like the little stray cat I was and made me a Rifton Academy elite right alongside them. I'm proud to call them my friends.

Bash is my first look into the people Luca has chosen to surround himself with—and I'm surprised to find out I don't hate what I'm seeing.

"You look like you're about to have an aneurysm." Bash chuckles, lifting the whisk to check the batter's consistency. "What's got your lips twisted like that?"

I raise a playful brow and deflect. "So I have you guys to thank for the one-eighty in Luca's personality?"

Bash brushes off his shoulder as if to congratulate himself. "I like to think so, but we can't take all the credit."

Rabid for more information, I shift to the edge of my seat and press. "Then what changed?"

Bash spins away from me and turns on one of the stove's six burners. "That's a story for him to tell."

Tension leaves my shoulders at his anticlimactic answer.

Well, shit.

Bash looks over his shoulder, his lips painted up in a smart-ass smirk.

He knows exactly what he's doing. Giving me just enough that I'm practically salivating over every bit of information I can get about Luca, and then withholding the good stuff.

I lift my chin and pretend I'm not completely annoyed. "I see. Then can you at least tell me what Bucket List Christmas is?"

Bash raises a brow as if to say, *now you're asking the right question* and offers me a wicked grin.

"That, I can do."

Chapter Eight

LEIGH

"There's no fucking way."

"No, seriously, I've never seen someone sing *Santa Baby* while decorating a tree better than Luca in a string bikini."

"I can corroborate the story," Holt adds, crossing his finger in an X over his heart—a solemn promise. It's an almost laughable sight coming from the-wall-of-muscle of an ex-hockey player. He joined us about halfway through Bash's explanation of Bucket List Christmas and was all too eager to dish the dirt on Luca, claiming he shouldn't have hidden me from them because I'm cool as shit.

His words, not mine.

Where Bash is a solid wall of muscles and Luca and Enzo are lean and defined, Holt is somewhere in the middle. His red hair and pale, freckled skin are absolutely the standout in the otherwise dark featured group, but it suits him as the hotheaded teeth collector of the group.

"And this was in Bali?" I clarify, mentally taking notes of all the places Bash and Holt have mentioned spending Christmas with Luca and Enzo.

So far there's been: Belize, Bali, Dubai, Arizona, Thailand, Sydney and Iceland.

Holt nods and snatches a piece of bacon from the plate in the middle of the island. "The first time, yes."

"There was more than once?" I choke, the visual of Luca in a string bikini both making me laugh and forcing me to clench my thighs at the same time.

I know what he's packing, and that outfit would absolutely leave little to the imagination.

"What can I say?" Bash shrugs and delivers another three pancakes from the griddle to Holt's plate. "Tequila makes that man's clothes fall off. It also entices him to make rather interesting bets. You can't blame us for taking advantage."

It amazes me the four of them have been doing this every Christmas for the last seven years. New locations and new adventures, each of them juggling professional careers while Enzo managed their portfolios. It's mind blowing.

Then again, as someone who doesn't have any immediate family to celebrate with, it sounds ideal. Especially now that Willow has Bishop and his eleven brothers and sisters to celebrate with. And Indie is generally gone, shooting whatever movie she's appearing in next. I foresee many Christmases that will be just Zach and me.

And maybe Luca.

I push the ghost of a thought away and focus on the two men in front of me. I can't help but wonder if their families miss them. Notably the Donatis, who never miss the chance to show off their perfect family.

My stomach flips when I think of Luca and Enzo's mother, Isabella Donati, and her lips pursed and judgmental stare. There is no way she's ever going to accept Zach. Not when I'm his mother.

So much for the dream of family Christmases.

"You're thinking too hard again," Bash chastises, pushing the plate of bacon in my direction. "This trip is about relaxing, not working."

Unease runs through me and a sarcastic laugh bubbles from the back of my throat. "Well, I was brought here under false pretenses, then."

And I'm definitely not one to slow down and relax. Nowadays, the one time a year I let myself let loose is for Willow's Birthday Palooza. Even then, the last one ended up being far less relaxing than anticipated.

"I still can't believe he lied to all of us." Holt leans over to check the monitor where Zach is still sleeping soundly.

At least one of us is making the most out of this vacation. The flight, plus fighting bedtime, must have really tired him out because usually he's up before the sun. Not that I'm complaining. It's nice getting more than five minutes of uninterrupted adult time. And I'm learning so much about Luca that I'm sure he'd never let slip.

"Okay then," I say, clasping my hands in front of me on the island. My gaze darts between Holt and Bash like I'm conducting an interview. Or maybe it's more of an interrogation. "So who picks where you guys go for Bucket List Christmas?"

"We take turns picking from a list." Holt glances over at Bash as he answers, and I get the feeling there's more to the story.

"And who made the list?"

The two of them look at each other again, as if they are afraid to say too much.

"Jack." Holt's eyes track toward the window, a hollow sadness taking over them.

I look at Bash, still trying to figure out what I'm missing, but he's already glanced away, too, his flirtatious demeanor long gone.

"Who's Jack?" I ask softly.

Holt gives Bash a small but encouraging nod.

"He's the fifth in our little group."

I'm hesitant to ask where he is, given the avoidance from these two usually forthcoming guys. So I play it safe and smirk. "Don't tell me he owns a soccer team."

"Actually, Jack was a golfer," Holt mutters, a weak smile splitting his lips to hide the hurt in his eyes.

I know that look. It's the look of someone who has loved and lost. It's pain and joy as you mourn and remember them at the same time. It's two sides of a coin you wish you never picked up.

Still, my morbid curiosity gets the best of me. "Was?"

Bash's lips press into a thin line. "We all lived together in college. Jack passed away our senior year."

"I'm so sorry." The words tumble from my mouth out of habit, even though I know damn well they don't make a lick of a difference.

Bash grimaces at the same time as Holt thanks me and takes over. "This trip is how we honor him. We found the list when we were cleaning out his room at the house. It was all the places he'd hoped to visit."

I'm fairly certain my heart melts. "That's unexpectedly sweet."

"We might be a bunch of jock assholes," Bash defends playfully, grasping the space over his heart like I wounded him, "but we're not all bad."

No. They're not. Though, I get the feeling that was more so directed at me and my view of Luca and not him and Holt.

I hate that he's right. I hate even more that I'm slowly becoming convinced of what everyone but me knows to be true.

Luca might not be as bad as I remember him. And I'm not entirely sure how that makes me feel.

I open my mouth to reassure Bash I don't think they're assholes, but before I utter a single syllable, Luca's voice booms through the kitchen.

"Where the hell is Zach?"

Then again, maybe it's better if I hold off on any rash judgment where Luca is concerned.

All three of us turn to see Luca standing in the mudroom doorway with his twin. It's amazing how two men with the same genetics can look so similar and yet so different at the same time.

Where Luca has a commanding, posh air about him in his designer jeans, white Henley and fitted navy peacoat, Enzo is more understated and relaxed in washed denim and a hoodie. Luca stands confident with his shoulders back whereas Enzo lingers back, looking past his brother like he'd rather be in the shadows.

They might wear the same face. But what does it say about me that my eyes linger far too long on the confident asshole with a desire to tame him instead of the safe, quiet brother?

"Whoa. Settle down, Dad of the Year." Holt snickers. "Leigh's got him pulled up on the nanny cam. He's exhausted, so she let him sleep and we've been watching to see when he wakes up."

Luca glances down at my phone, locking in on the image of my son sleeping. Seconds pass as he continues to watch and I can't help but wonder if, like me, he's waiting to catch the steady rise and fall of Zach's chest.

Once he's satisfied, Luca leans against the island with both hands and drags his stony glare back to me. "What are you even doing in here?"

"Good morning to you, too," I greet, lifting my mug in his direction. When he doesn't do more than deadpan, I continue, "I needed coffee, and then Bash was nice enough to make me breakfast."

Luca scowls at Bash as he rounds the island and picks up a pancake and takes a bite. "It's not your job to feed her."

"Maybe if you did," Bash mutters.

"I never got the chance," Luca snaps, and the pointed glower he gives Bash has him raising his hands in surrender and quitting while he's ahead.

I roll my eyes and lay on a thick layer of sweetness in my voice. "Don't listen to him, Bash. You can feed me these fluffy slices of heaven any time you'd like." Stabbing my fork into a pancake, I make a show of dipping it into syrup and slowly bring it to my mouth.

Luca's eyes track my movement and flash with something that could either be desire or hatred, though if I had to guess, it's the latter.

It shouldn't be so satisfying that getting along with his friends gets under his skin—but it really is.

I swallow and smile. "Holt and Bash were just telling me about Bucket List Christmas."

"Well, they shouldn't," Luca grumbles as he and his brother round the island and load up their plates with pancakes and bacon.

I shrug. "I think it's sweet you guys do this. I—"

"No one asked you," Luca snaps, cutting me off.

"*Damn*, Luca. Who pissed in your Cheerios?"

Luca grunts in Holt's general direction as he slides into the seat farthest away from me, but it sounds a whole lot like, "She did."

My eyes dart between the four men sitting at the island. Holt and Bash glare at Luca, who is giving as good as he's getting. Enzo, on the other hand, grins like a kid in a damn candy store, watching this all unfold. I get the feeling he might be a chaos gremlin at heart.

"Aaand on that note, I'm going to head back to the guesthouse." I press my hands onto the counter and leverage myself up.

The second I take a step, Luca shoots up from his seat and, abandoning his food, heads toward the door. "Good, we need to talk before we head out."

I freeze. "We?"

"I've got plans with the guys today and need to speak with you beforehand." He jerks his head back toward the island.

"The only plans I have today are with the hot tub on that deck," Bash counters. "My muscles are killing me from yesterday."

"Suck it up, cupcake. The trail riders called," Enzo explains. "The weather is better today for the horses. So if we want to see the mountains up close, today is the day."

Holt shouts, "Yee haw," while circling his hand over his head like he's roping cattle.

In response, Bash starts on about how he'd be a much better cowboy than Holt because he grew up on a vineyard with horses. Holt vehemently disagrees, pointing out he went to Boy Scout camp once and was an excellent rider. They go back and forth and a minute later, there is a bet in place to see which of them is the better cowboy on their outing today.

It's endearing and wholesome, and I can't help but roll my eyes.

Fucking men.

Thankfully, their discussion serves as the perfect moment for me to slip out while Luca is distracted.

I'm inches from the door to the mudroom when Enzo calls out, "Why don't you come with us, Leigh?"

See? Chaos gremlin.

I stop in the doorway and look over my shoulder. "Uh, no, you guys go. I've got stuff I can work on, and I've got Zach to worry about." My gaze lands on Bash and I smile. "Thanks for breakfast."

He lifts his hand in a mock salute. "Anytime, Baby Momma."

"Do not call her that," Luca growls before spinning on his heel to follow me.

And to think I was so close to avoiding him.

"Let me know if you get that stick out of his ass," Holt hollers.

"I didn't know it could be removed," I mutter loud enough for them to hear me, relishing in the laughter from Enzo, Holt, and Bash just as much as the exasperated sigh that comes from Luca.

The sun breaks over the mountain, causing the snow remnants on the deck to glitter as Luca follows me toward the guest house.

His footsteps behind me stop before I reach the door, and I turn around to face him.

"I sent off the test this morning," he says before I can start.

Ah, so that's why he's already in such a foul mood.

I lift my phone and check the time. "It's only eight thirty. How did you manage that?"

"I drove it to the airport so it would be on the first flight out to a facility I trust," he says it as if it's the simplest thing in the world. Like anyone could just snap their fingers and make it happen.

Releasing a weighted sigh, I meet his icy blue gaze, praying he hears me when I tell him, "I'm not here to screw you, Luca. If you're Zach's father, then I want him to know you. I—"

He throws up a hand, stopping me. "Listen, I don't have the time to get into everything right now, and I'm pretty sure I'm still too angry to talk about all this between us. I just wanted you to know it's been sent."

I hold his stare but ultimately give in. As much as I want him to understand that I'm not the bad guy, he just told me he's not ready to talk, and I have to respect that.

"Thank you for your honesty."

Luca nods and pulls out a folded-over manila envelope from the pocket of his peacoat and offers it to me. "Here's the Monarch Hearts stuff for you to look over while we're gone today."

I take the folder and slide out the paper clipped stack of papers. It doesn't take me more than a few moments to flip through it.

My jaw drops, unable to process what I'm seeing. "Luca, this is a full proposal ready to be presented to the commissioner."

"I know."

I don't need to look up to know he's wearing a smug smile.

Looking deeper into the document, my voice goes high. "It even has the section I add to each one for team specific ideas."

This must have taken him hours and a shit ton of forethought to put together. Usually it takes an entire week of sitting down with a team and hashing out all the mandatories, wish lists, and what we can and can't make happen for each club.

But Luca has thought of everything. I mean, of course I still need to do a deep dive and make sure, but on the surface, it looks better than even something I could have come up with.

It's immaculate.

"Phillip let me take a look at his proposal," Luca explains, like he didn't go unnecessarily above and beyond. "You just need to look over it and approve it."

I don't bother hiding my shock. "How—I mean, why would you do this?"

Luca gives a sheepish pop of his shoulders, his confidence wavering. Though I don't miss the glint of pride in his eyes. "I figured we'd have more important things to talk about."

"This is—it's impressive."

"Thanks."

Time passes like molasses. Each of us awkwardly staring at the other, neither of us knowing how to maintain this moment of peace without ruining it.

Luca runs a nervous hand through his jet-black hair. "I, uh—better get going. We can discuss it after you have a chance to thoroughly rip it apart."

A sarcastic remark sits on the tip of my tongue, but I bite it back. He deserves this win for all the work he put in.

"I'm sure it's amazing." The compliment sticks to the roof of my mouth, but I mean every word.

Luca nods and turns toward the house. He takes two steps before he stops and his shoulders slump forward with the weight of a sigh. Turning back around, his crystal blue eyes connect with mine, this time soft like snow instead of sharpened into ice daggers. "Since the proposal is done, would you like to come with us?"

I might as well be a fish out of water with the way my mouth gapes. If I wasn't caught off guard by his question, the emotional whiplash would have killed me.

"Is this you speechless?" Luca chuckles. "Because I think it's my second favorite view of you."

"Do I even want to know the first?"

He shrugs. "It might surprise you."

"I doubt that," I say, shaking my head. I absolutely do not need a reminder that he's seen me face down, ass up. "Thank you for the offer, but I should read through this proposal. And I've got Zach to think about."

Luca closes the space between us in two of his long strides and grabs the proposal from my hand.

"Hey!" I try to grab it back, but I've got nothing on his six-foot-four wingspan.

"You can have it back later." Luca folds it back over and shoves it back in his pocket. "Does Zach have a jacket and snow pants?"

"Well yeah, but—"

"Do you?"

"Yes, but—"

"Then you are both set. He'll love it, and I get the feeling you don't take a lot of time to slow down and take in nature."

Nature, yes. Spending half the summer at the Renegades Hearts summer camp up in upstate New York, I am well acquainted with nature. Though he might have a point when it comes to slowing down.

Still, with all the uncertainty between us, I'm not sure it's a good idea.

Luca smiles, waiting for my answer and my stomach flips in a way it has no business doing.

Why couldn't he have been smug and ugly instead of confident and gorgeous?

In a desperate attempt to regain some semblance of control, I cross my hands over my chest and dig my heels in. "I thought you said you were too angry to be around me."

He nods. "I'm still too upset to talk about co-parenting, but I'm pretty sure I can manage being around you for the day if you think you can."

I cock a brow.

"What if I promise not to talk about the paternity test, or Zach's parentage?"

"Considering the way you bit my head off back in the kitchen, I'm not sure I believe you."

He mutters a string of curses under his breath, and for a moment, I think he's about to give up his quest.

Instead, he doubles down.

"Today is supposed to be about celebrating life and friendship. Even you and your type A perfectionism can understand that. Plus, we both know spending the day with us will be more fun than reading a proposal and staying cooped up in the guest house."

He's clearly never spent time with an almost two-year-old, because there is no way I am going to keep that kid cooped up. I've already looked up every park within walking distance of the rental.

"Plus, Zach will love seeing the horses."

Damn him for resorting to using my son's obsession with horses against me. Which he only knows because my best friend couldn't keep her mouth shut.

"I'm still—"

"Just say yes, Leigh."

I don't want to.

I really don't.

Because if I do, I might learn more about this man. As it is, I'm already having a hard time keeping the lines of past and present from blurring.

But he's right. Zach will love seeing the horses.

And this is about him.

Which is why, despite shaking my head in defeat, I reluctantly agree. "Fine."

"That's not a yes."

This man is infuriating. And kind. And I don't know what the hell to think anymore. One minute he's reminding me that I'm the world's shittiest human being for keeping secrets, and the next he's making my insides melt with his thoughtfulness—both toward Zach and me.

My lips move before I can stop them. "Yes."

"Great." Luca clasps his hands together, and I swear I see his mind moving a million miles a minute. "I'm going to call the wranglers and let them know that we'll take the sleigh in addition to the trail horses. We leave in an hour. Will that be enough time to get Zach ready?"

Anxiety slithers up my spine, but it's accompanied by a hint of excitement.

I nod. "I'll meet you out front."

"Perfect."

He pulls out his phone, and I turn back to the guest house. As my hand twists the doorknob, Luca calls my name.

"Oh, and Leigh?"

I look over my shoulder and see he's at the mudroom door. "Yeah?"

"My friends are off limits."

This presumptuous jackass.

"No need to be jealous. Asshole jocks aren't my type."

Luca's chest shakes with a deep chuckle as he pushes into the main house. "If you say so."

"I do," I whisper to myself.

Though I'm not sure who I'm trying to convince more—him or me.

Chaper Nine

LUCA

My ass is sore.

And not from the stick Leigh and my friends assume is perpetually stuck there.

Why Enzo thought it was a good idea to ride horses…in the snow… for thirty minutes, just to have brisket and beer with a view of the mountains Jack wanted to visit (solely because they were on the can of his favorite light beer) I'm not sure. We might all be ex-pro athletes who have stayed decently in shape, but I'm fairly certain nothing could have prepared our bodies for this.

I shift in the saddle, trying to hide my discomfort.

Holt chuckles from atop his horse as he slides up next to me.

"I take it I'm not the only one who will be utilizing that hot tub tonight."

"And every night from now till New Year," I mutter. "You know Jack would love this shit and is probably laughing hysterically at us right now."

"No doubt." Holt huffs, his voice weighted with the sadness we all feel every year we do this without our friend. It's both heartbreaking and refreshing and not something I would trade for anything in the world.

"How are you holding up?"

I side-eye Holt, brow raised. "Can I assume you're not talking about my ass in this saddle?"

He jerks his head in the direction of the sleigh, gliding along the wide snow-laden trail to our left, and I follow his gaze.

Zach is giggling in his mother's lap, pointing at the horses pulling the carriage. Leigh has her head tipped back, laughing at something the ranch hand steering the sleigh said.

If I had known they were going to send the Captain America of cowboys, I wouldn't have asked Leigh to join us. Or at the very least, I would have opted to ride in the sleigh with them. Instead, I had the brilliant idea to ride this damn horse to impress Zach. Now I'm learning the hard way almost two-year-olds don't give a shit about things like that. There's also the realization that as much as I don't like Leigh flirting with my friends, I really don't like her flirting with random strangers on romantic sleigh rides.

"I'm not going to ask again." Holt adds, "You didn't give us much to go on last night, but anyone with eyes can see you're spiraling. I'm just not sure if it's towards something good or bad."

It's such a Holt response. Never pushing too hard or fighting for answers. He's a firm believer in if you want to, you will.

"Is there a good spiral?" I ask, which earns me a pointed glare.

He's not wrong. I feel like I'm a spinning top, bouncing off every wall in sight, waiting for gravity to stop me and make sense of the emotions swirling in my chest.

Last night I was too angry to give them more than the basics: Leigh and I were old acquaintances who fucked in a hotel vending machine room and may or may not have a child together. I left out the part where I ruined her life as a teenager, but they know that story and put two and two together, thanks to Enzo. Thankfully, they got the hint I didn't want to talk and didn't pry further. And I didn't give them the opportunity this morning. Mostly because I'm still trying to reconcile how I was okay with her not telling me about Zach as long as I got to be a part of his life, but now that I might not be his father, I'm ready to rage.

Then there's the fact that the sight of Leigh, with her cute freckles, blonde curls, and leggings that have no business being so damn tight, makes me harder than a fucking rock at the most inopportune moments.

Like now.

But there's no way I'm admitting that to Holt. He'd never let me live it down that I—Bash's playboy wingman—is hard at the mere sight of a woman.

The rest, though, he might understand.

I shift in my saddle and exhale deep from my lungs. "I thought I knew what I wanted. Now I'm not sure if it's possible."

"But you want her?"

As if it's that simple.

"No. Yes." I hesitate, trying to pinpoint exactly what it is I want, even though I know damn well what sparked a fire in my soul. I glance from the trail ahead over at Holt, my lips in a solemn line. "I want a family."

If he's shocked, his face doesn't reveal it. The damn stoic bastard. If he isn't raging, he's practically the Dalai Lama. It's unnerving.

Not that I expect him to be caught off guard. I might not have explicitly shared my want of a family, but the guys know how much I cherish what we have. They are my brothers as much as my twin is.

But it's not the same.

There is something about the idea of family, one that is entirely mine and of my making. They can be everything I never had. And I can give them everything I've always wanted. Because that's the thing about having your heart broken by the people who are supposed to always stand by your side. You learn what you won't settle for and create the life you deserve.

I deserve to know my son.

I deserve a partner who will stand by my side.

Just like Zach deserves to have two parents who love him and remind him every fucking day he is the center of their world.

Holt's lips give a slight purse and gently tugs on the reins to slow down, creating more room between us and the sleigh. "That's what you really want?"

"I didn't know until the opportunity was thrust into my lap, but yeah," I admit, tugging on my own reins to keep pace with him.

"Have you told Leigh?"

I wince. "Not exactly."

I'm pretty sure she would be on the first flight out of here if she was aware of all the things I want with her.

"And you haven't apologized yet."

"No." The word is strained through gritted teeth, the weight of exactly how ass backwards I've handled the situation heavy on my chest. "I wasn't expecting there to be a chance Zach wasn't mine."

"Ahhh." Holt nods, all the pieces clicking together. "You got ahead of yourself again."

"All in, all the time," I say with a grin, but it's a cover for all the times my impulsive nature has bitten me in the ass.

Holt laughs. "We really need to get you to stop sticking your giant ass foot in your mouth."

"Don't I know it?" I huff, disheartened. "I just feel like I got a taste of what I could have and then she ripped it away from me. And now I'm having to learn to live with the fact it might not have ever been mine. I want it to be mine." With each statement, my voice grows louder and Holt glances toward the sleigh to make sure we aren't being overheard, but I don't care. I keep going. "How the hell could she do that to me? She's known where I am. Hell, I saw her this past summer, and she said nothing. We could've been a family. I could've—"

Fuck.

My nose and throat burn as I choke on my words. This was not supposed to be a cathartic breakdown in the middle of the woods, but I think Holt knew I needed it. Especially if I'm going to spend the day playing nice with Leigh.

"And you still want to be a family?"

"Yes," I answer without a second thought. "If Zach is mine, I want to be a part of his life."

"What about Leigh?"

I consider his question, glancing at the blonde from the corner of my eye.

Do I want Leigh?

Sexually? Yes. Always. I wasn't kidding when I said she gives the best head I've ever received. She's also got this commanding side that makes my dick hard. I've never wanted to explore that with someone, but with her—the things I'd let her do to me are endless.

But beyond that, do I want Leigh?

What do I really know about her?

When she was young, she was feisty but brought sunshine into every room she entered. There wasn't a trace of the walls she's erected to keep people out.

Now she's the CFO of Renegade Hearts and has done amazing things there. She's smart. Loyal. And she can clearly keep up with Bash and Holt, so she's got that going for her. Most importantly, she puts Zach first and is an incredible mom.

This is all assuming we can go five minutes without finding a reason to tear each other apart.

Not that I don't find that incredibly endearing, because I do.

But is that enough to want forever with her?

I know the answer, but admitting it out loud is not something I'm prepared to do. Not when I'm already struggling to protect my heart. Leigh could absolutely be it for me. Mine in every way, shape and form.

And the way I'm okay with that scares the shit out of me. Because for every thought of us being a family, there's one where she doesn't forgive me, and I'm forced to sit by and watch Zach live a life with parents who can't coexist.

So I shrug nonchalantly and grin. "I mean, I could do worse."

"Luca," Holt deadpans, making it clear I'm not getting out of this with my charming wit or dignity intact.

"Fine," I grunt. "Possibly."

It's not the answer he's looking for, but it's not a lie.

"So what are you going to do about it?"

"That's the million-dollar question, isn't it?"

Going into the weekend, I was so sure I had the perfect plan. Now—not so much.

Holt presses his lips together, a signature move he does when he's trying to figure out how to let you down easy. "You aren't going to like what I'm about to say."

And there it is.

"If you tell me you'll fight me for her, I'll knock you off that horse and make it look like an accident when you break your neck."

Holt tips his head back and laughs. It's loud enough that Zach and Leigh turn around to see what the commotion is. She arches a brow but goes back to talking to Brad or Chad, or whatever the pretty cowboy said his name was.

"Maybe if she was my type, but we both know that's not the case."

No, Holt might not discriminate against the sexes when it comes to people in his bed, but he tends to like them without a single thought between their ears. The last guy he kept around for more than a few weeks thought they painted the yellow down lines on the football field between each play.

"What I was going to say is she's one of the good ones."

I snort and fist the reins in frustration. "You'd know better than me. It's not like we did a lot of talking the last time she spent more than five minutes in my presence."

"Your asshole is showing," he says, rolling his eyes.

He's right. It's a deflection. I know she's exactly the kind of woman I'd share the rest of my life with. It's true that I don't know who she is now, but I can't believe she's fundamentally a different person. The problem is, if I'm not Zach's father, it might be a moot point because she still hates me.

Aside from Enzo, Holt probably knows me better than any of the guys in the group.

"All I'm saying is don't let it or your past blind you to what's right in front of you."

"Next thing you know, you're going to be speaking ass backwards like Yoda."

"There is no try, only do."

I grab the rolled blanket behind my saddle and chuck it at him. For a moment, I regret it, considering we're on horses and I'm pretty sure it's not advisable to spook them. Thankfully, Holt catches it and neither of the horses seems bothered by my antics. They keep following the sleigh like it's their only job in the world.

We make the rest of the ride in silence, and I get lost in replaying every interaction with Leigh since she arrived.

It's short-lived because as we round the next bend in the trail, the forest gives way to an open meadow nestled at the foot of a range of mountains. In the center is a cabin with white smoke billowing from the chimney. It's like something straight out of a fairytale.

But that's not what snags my attention.

It's the smile on the gorgeous blonde in the sleigh and the single tear dripping down her face.

It's the twinkle in Zach's eyes as he watches Bash and Enzo gallop ahead with our guide.

It's a feeling I can't explain. But somehow, I know this is where I'm supposed to be.

And it's right then I realize just how fucking screwed I am.

Because it's not just a possibility of wanting this with Leigh.

It's an absolute.

Now I just have to convince her to give me a chance to prove I can be everything Zach needs.

And hopefully something she needs too.

Chapter Ten

LEIGH

I clutch the piece of paper with Bradley's number in my fist and do my best to hide the stupid grin on my face. There's not a world in which I'll be calling the incredibly sexy cowboy, but it's been a long time since a man has taken an interest in me after knowing I have a kid. Usually when they find out, men come up with a convenient reason to run in the opposite direction.

Bradley didn't. In fact, he seemed keen to scoop Zach up and teach him to be a real cowboy. It was freaking adorable. What made it even better was the utter dismay of my broody, maybe-baby-daddy. If looks could kill, Luca would be on his way to jail for first degree murder.

I don't need that kind of karma on my conscience. Which is why, for the moment, this number will remain nothing but an incredible confidence booster and a reminder that maybe I won't have to die all alone. Someday the timing will be right, and the right guy will want to share a life with Zach and me. Ideally, he'll also live in New York and not on a rural farm in the mountains of Colorado. But you know, beggars can't be choosers, so maybe I could get used to the rustic life.

"Hey," Luca calls out as I cross the deck and look out over at him and the three other guys building snowmen with Zach.

Bash and Holt are creating what looks like an anatomically correct snow lady, while Luca and Enzo are showing Zach how to shape snow on what looks more like a dilapidated volcano than a snowman.

And damn, is my boy grinning.

Leaning over the railing, Zach's giggle warms my soul. "That's a mighty fine snowman."

Holt and Bash look up, their hands each cupping their snow woman's double D tits. "Why thank you."

I roll my eyes and slide my gaze back to Zach, who is shoving a piece of snow in his mouth.

Luca follows my line of sight and chuckles. "At least it's not yellow."

"He's probably getting hungry." I glance down at my watch and see it's already past noon.

Luca's eyes widen and he whips his head back to Zach, who is enjoying every bite of his wild snow cone. "Shit, I'm sorry. I should have thought about that. When does he usually eat?"

"A half hour ago," I admit. "But there's no way you could've known. I'll just run up and see how much longer till the food is ready."

"I'll go with you." Luca drops the snow in his hand and gives Enzo a silent look, asking if he's got Zach. His twin nods.

They've done the twin telepathy a few times today, and each time it sends a pang through my heart. I never had siblings, but how amazing it must be to have someone who, no matter what, just gets it. They're always on your side and know what you're thinking without a single word needing to be said.

In a few short strides, Luca's hopping the deck railing and at my side. I'm about to insist I can do it myself, but he doesn't give me the chance. He invades my space and my senses with his broad frame and musky cologne. His perfectly sculpted brow is raised as he looks down his nose at me.

"For the record, I know you could do it yourself. I wanted to talk to you before we eat."

"Oh." I wasn't expecting that. Usually he's all *Me Tarzan, You Jane. You do what I say.* But once again, just like with all he's done for Zach and Monarch Hearts, he's surprised me with thoughtfulness.

Seriously, who is this man?

Luca's eyes trail down, lingering first on my lips, then lower to my puffer jacket. His gaze skates along the curve where breast meets waist. It's slow. Deliberate. And it's turning my body into a wanton traitor.

I struggle to suppress the shiver that slithers down my spine and straight to my core.

That didn't happen when Bradley looked at me like that.

"And in case no one has told you, teal suits you." The way he says it—relaxed, eyes heated, and ending with his lower lip caught between his teeth—is more than friendly, but not quite romantic.

At the moment, it's too much for my brain to process. Which is why I only manage to mutter a weak, "Uh, thanks."

If Luca notices the pink in my cheeks, he doesn't say before he turns on his heel and heads for the cabin.

I'm left standing there trying to get my back-stabbing body under control. I'm definitely not supposed to be noticing the way his designer snow pants hug his ass and thighs. The man might not play baseball anymore, but damn, all those years at shortstop did wonders for his backside.

God, what is wrong with me? This is Luca Donati. The man who ruined my life. Who manipulated us into showing up for this trip when we really didn't need to.

But he's also the man who picked out all my son's favorites. And finished our entire proposal on his own so I wouldn't have to worry about it while we were here.

"Leigh, you coming?"

Luca's voice pulls me from my spiraling thoughts, and I glance up to find him standing with his head poked out from the cabin door.

"Yeah."

I follow Luca inside where Martha, the sweet matriarch of the farm, is putting the finishing touches on what looks like a broccoli salad.

The moment she sees Luca and me, she smiles. "You two have the sweetest little boy. He reminds me so much of my grandson, Ryan."

"Oh, he's not—"

"Thank you," Luca cuts me off with a smug smile. "He's definitely something special."

Apparently, I didn't need to spiral. Just give Luca another thirty seconds and he would have reminded me why I hate him on his own.

I pin a glare in his direction, and the bastard shrugs like it's no big deal. But it is.

Each moment Zach and I spend here, I feel like I'm losing everything I have fought so hard to protect. And to make matters worse, I'm losing it to someone who has no idea how special it is. We're just a shiny toy right now. But what happens when we have to actually parent? When it's not just a fun trip to the mountains. Will Luca show up then?

I swallow hard past the lump in my throat and look past him at Martha. "No rush, but when will lunch be ready? I'm trying to make sure we don't end up with a hangry toddler."

"Oh!" Martha exclaims in the way only a fretful grandmother can. "I completely understand, darling. Here, if you want to have him start with some fruit, I've got a bowl chopped and ready." She turns around and pulls a bowl of berries from a vintage refrigerator. Setting down on the edge of the worn chopping block, she pushes it toward us.

"Thank you so much," I say, making a note to see if the Denver Hearts chapter would consider partnering with this family-owned business for future fun outings. It would definitely be a trek out here, but the kids would love the horses. The trail ride to the hundred-year-old cabin where Martha and her family cook a homemade meal for guests and tell them all about the history of the land would be both heartwarming and breathtaking.

Luca grabs the fruit with one hand while his other slips to my lower back.

Martha's gaze tracks his movement, and she offers me a sly wink as Luca gently steers me back toward the door we came through.

The moment we are out of sight of the sweet old woman who thinks we're the poster family for cuteness, I spin on him.

"What the hell was that?"

Luca chuckles but keeps walking until he reaches the railing, then calls Enzo over to grab the fruit to offer Zach.

It's not until he's done that he looks back and realizes I'm still waiting for an answer.

"What's the harm in letting a little old woman—who we will never see again, I might add—believe we're a family?"

"You can't seriously be this dense." I push a stray curl from my face, tucking it behind my ear. "You know who you are, right?"

He saunters back over to where to me and crosses his arms over his broad chest, a barrier of defense. "I'm fairly certain I remember my name."

My eyes widen, surprised he's still not getting it.

"Luca, the four of you are owners of major league franchises, not to mention four of the most eligible bachelors in sports."

He raises a brow and grins. "So you've been doing your research on us."

"You think I would let my son build snowmen with strangers?"

"No, you're too good a mom for that."

His compliment catches me off guard, and I tumble over my words. "I—Thank you. But you must realize all it would take is one phone call and your name, along with mine, and Zach will be plastered all over *The*

Foul Line."

I've made it a point to stay off the radar of the trashy sports news sight. I don't need anyone speculating who my son belongs to or commenting on me raising him as a single mom. It hasn't been easy with all the coverage of Willow taking over as the Renegades owner and Renegade Hearts getting the official MLB sponsorship, but somehow I've managed.

Then again, if Luca is his dad, it's only a matter of time.

"I really don't think Martha has a cellphone, let alone is going to call *The Foul Line*, but you're right and I'm sorry."

Compliments and apologies.

Who the hell is this man and what has he done with the asshole who can't help but fight me?

"But honestly, it's Chad the Cowboy you should be worried about."

Ah, there he is.

"Your jealousy is showing," I tease, narrowing my gaze as I prepare to go for the kill. "Bradley signed an NDA."

His haughty grin falters. "What?"

"When we arrived, I had him and the other trail riders sign an NDA that they wouldn't discuss any of us with the media. I just haven't had the chance to have the rest of the staff at the house do the same."

"Why would you do that?" His voice is a low, borderline menacing tone, as if I'm the one who did something wrong.

"Because, unlike the four of you, I have someone else to think about other than myself." The way his face falls when I twist the knife I buried in his chest almost has me feeling bad.

I don't actually think Martha is going to do anything with the knowledge. Luca is right. She's old and couldn't care less who we are. But a part of me just needed to prove a point.

He's in over his head with Zach and me. Especially when he has no idea if Zach is even his. There are precautions that need to be taken. Having Zach's favorites and writing a proposal isn't enough.

Luca looks over his shoulder to where Zach is playing with his twin, a look like I just kicked his puppy etched on his face.

Damn it.

I didn't mean to fuck this up.

Or maybe I did.

Why does this have to be so complicated?

Searching for safe waters, I step forward and change the topic. "You said you wanted to talk to me?"

"I did." Luca turns and rests his elbows on the railing, gesturing for me to join him.

I do, and the two of us look out at where Zach is snacking with Enzo, while Holt and Bash are using the raspberries to give their snow woman nipples.

Fucking men.

"I'm sorry for how I reacted last night," Luca starts. "And for telling Martha we were a family."

I sigh. "Me too."

"You were just trying to protect Zach."

"That's all I'm ever trying to do."

There's a stretch of silence, and Luca keeps his eyes locked on Zach like he's trying to memorize every inch of him. "I just feel like I've missed so much."

Luca hangs his head, and guilt smacks me across the face. Hard. I know I'm the asshole here, even if I only ever had the best of intentions. There's a part of me that wishes I could give him my memories of all the big and small moments, while the other, larger part of me wants to scream, *you don't even know if he's yours.*

The first isn't possible, and the second isn't productive.

Luca knows the facts, but it's the limbo we're stuck in that's hard.

Hugging him seems too personal, and words are nothing more than hollow sounds, but I want him to know I get it and I'm sorry.

Putting on my big girl panties, I scoot closer to him until my shoulder and bicep touch his. It's simple and can't be construed as intimate in any way, shape, or form. "I'm sorry I never told you. I should have."

"Thank you for that," Luca says, leaning into my touch, and I melt just a little.

"I wish I knew where we go from here," I start softly, testing this uncharted moment of peaceful honesty between us. "I'm trying to be okay with being here. And like I said, if you're his father, I won't keep him from you. Zach will always be my top priority."

"Me too. Always." It's an instant reaction, one with the weight of a promise behind it. Luca lifts his head and swivels it toward me. "Can we start over?"

It's a loaded question.

He searches my face for an answer, but I can't give it to him, because I don't have one.

"I don't know," I admit. "Too much has happened. I mean, of course, for Zach, we will figure out how to co-parent but—I don't think you understand the way you hurt me."

"I—"

I throw up a hand and stop him. "Don't tell me you're sorry. I know you are. You've made it clear you want to apologize for everything. But those are just words."

Hollow. Empty. Meaningless without action.

"Then let me show you."

Once again, he catches me off guard and I jerk back, brow raised. "You want to show me?"

"Absolutely."

"How?"

His blue eyes lock on mine, filled with determination I didn't expect. "Stay."

"Where?" I play stupid because I know he didn't just ask me to stay in Telluride.

"Here." He reaches out and grabs my hand. "Don't leave tomorrow. Stay here for Christmas."

My heart flutters, but I ignore the useless organ and latch onto reason, snatching my hand free of his. "Are you crazy? We can't do that. What about Bucket List Christmas? We've already intruded enough and everything I've gotten Zach for Christmas is in New York."

He huffs a laugh followed by a dramatic eye roll. "First of all, the guys love you guys. I'm sure they'd ask you to stay themselves."

I glance at where Holt and Bash have now joined Enzo and Zach, and the four of them are throwing berries up and trying to catch them in their mouths, sending my son into a fit of giggles.

I smile. "They love Zach. They tolerate me for your sake. But this is a special thing for you guys. We don't need to be here."

"Pshhh," Luca huffs. "I have it on good authority that if you weren't my baby momma, more than one of them would have already put the moves on you."

It's my turn to roll my eyes, biting my tongue to keep from reminding him we don't know I'm his baby momma. "Was it Bash?"

He smirks. "You think I'm going to tell you?"

Eyes narrowing, I smirk. "I'll get it out of them."

"You'll have to stay then," he surmises, smug like he's won the conversation.

"What about Zach's stuff?" I counter. "I might not be big on Christmas, but I promised to make it special."

"We're going to circle back to that, but as for Zach, I'll get the things sent here." He tilts his head playfully and smiles. "Plus, what's more special than Christmas in Telluride?"

"Christmas with the people who love him," I clap back.

Luca explodes, knocking snow from the railing as he slams his hand down. "We could love him if you let us!"

Three sets of eyes swing our direction, and I could kill Luca for putting me in this position. Each of the guys stare for a beat with nothing but pity in their gaze. Though I'm not sure if it's for me or Luca. Maybe both.

But for how long? How long will they stick around if I let them? Only until we find out the results of the paternity test? For Christmas? His birthday? What if Luca's not the father?

The guys awkwardly turn back to entertain Zach, and I shift my weight so I am facing Luca. He does the same, and I know we've reached the point where a decision has to be made.

"Luca, I—"

"Please, Leigh." He cuts me off. Eyes wide and pleading, my name is a prayer of desperation on his lips. "I've already missed so much. I know he might not be mine, but on the off chance he is, don't ask me to miss another Christmas."

Fuck.

He's right.

I hate that he's right.

But it doesn't make it any less true.

"Okay," I whisper, defeated and resolute.

Luca's brow raises. "Really?"

I give a shaky nod. "I can't argue with that. Zach is my world, and that sentiment goes both ways. He's missed that time with you too."

His arms shoot out, and before I can duck away, he tugs me against his chest. I try not to think about the way I fit perfectly beneath his chin as he lowers his head to the shell of my ear and whispers, "Thank you."

My head spins. His heady scent and strong arms mixed with this soft sentiment are too much for my brain to compute. "Uh, yeah. You're welcome."

He releases me and we both stand there, neither of us making a move to step away. I watch as Luca registers just how close, and I know I should be the one to step back. But ever the masochist of my own feelings, I don't.

He leans forward, ever so slightly, his chest brushing against mine and despite the layers of warming layers, my nipples tighten.

Nope.

He sucks his upper lip between his teeth and sucks in a sharp breath, and my eyes zero in on his lips.

So much fucking nope.

My body and all its cobwebs might want another taste of Luca, but there is not a chance in hell I'm going there.

At least that's what my brain is saying, but my body doesn't get the message.

He leans in further.

His lips centimeters from mine.

The ghost of a touch is there.

Of course, that's when my brain catches on and I force a cough, breaking the moment.

"I—I'm going to pee," I stammer, stumbling back. "Would you mind rounding up the guys for lunch?"

Luca hesitates, and a knowing grin splits the lips that were moments ago destined for mine. "Sure thing."

Turning on my heel, I take off for the cabin like a bat out of hell. Once I'm in the safety of the rickety old bathroom, I splash some water on my face as the weight of what just transpired sinks in.

We're staying.

Here.

With Luca.

Who I hate.

Who almost kissed me.

I reach up and trace my lower lip with my finger.

What the hell was I thinking agreeing to this?

And why do I wish I had stayed just a second longer?

Chapter Eleven

LUCA

Lunch with my best friends shouldn't be reminiscent of a high society party, but add in Leigh and Zach, and I feel like I'm back in Shady Grove, navigating one of my mother's mandatory holiday get-togethers. Except instead of gaudy Christmas outfits and meddling mothers trying to pair me off with their daughters, I'm up against Leigh's side-eye glances, checking to see if I'm taking care of Zach to her standards.

I couldn't believe it when she agreed to let me take the lead on lunch with Zach. She even made it a point to sit down at the opposite end of the table between Enzo and Holt.

Of course, that could also be her subtle attempt to put space between us.

A Cheshire cat grin splits my lips as I methodically cut Zach's roasted chicken and asparagus into tiny pieces while picturing his mother pressed up against me, my lips hovering over hers.

She felt something, too—if only for a moment—before she turned and ran. But it was there. And it gives me hope that maybe the idea of us being a family isn't as far-fetched as I thought.

Then again, we have a long way and a severely needed apology on my part before we get there.

I glance down at the towhead toddler beside me, offering him his plate.

He immediately reaches for the chicken with his hands, and for a moment, I consider letting him do so, mostly because I love that it's something that would irritate my mother. Then again, it could be a teaching moment. I can't help myself. This is what I wanted. To be his dad.

I pull his plate back toward me and pick up the fork from the table, offering it to him.

Zach looks at the fork, back up at me, and shakes his head. "No."

"Come on, little man," I coax, putting the fork closer to his hand. "We gotta use the fork."

"Shit," Leigh mutters, halting Bash's explanation to her on the benefits of a quarterback sneak. "I forgot to tell you he's not a big fan of utensils."

"Do you mind if I try getting him to use them?"

She hesitates, then lifts her hand and gestures for me to proceed, her lips pressed in a tight grin that says, *it's your funeral.*

Permission granted, I lean down so I'm on Zach's level and whisper, "You know, my brother didn't like forks when we were little either."

His little brows raise skeptically, but he keeps listening.

"Really." I point to where Enzo is sitting on the other side of Zach. "I used to have to feed Enzo, because our mom wouldn't let him touch his food with his hands."

Zach looks down at the fork and up at Enzo.

"It's true. Our mom would make Luca feed me, then I would have to feed him since he fed me all the food from his plate."

I look up at my brother and silently thank him for playing along and making my ass backwards logic make sense. Not that my almost two-year-old is understanding much of it.

"Would you like to try feeding me?" I ask Zach.

Now that he understood.

"Yes!" he cheers, like I've just given him permission to have candy before dinner.

He reaches over and awkwardly stabs a piece of chicken from his plate and reaches up, offering it to me.

My eyes fall in a longing glance at the ribs on my plate. I've been dreaming about them since Enzo booked this excursion for us—all smothered in homemade barbecue sauce, smoked low and slow for hours.

And now I'm settling for my kid's chicken.

There's got to be some bullshit parenting meme about this. If not, I'm going to make one.

A small laugh catches my attention. I look in the direction it came from and spot Leigh, hand covering her mouth. Tears are in her eyes, but also the hint of a smile just past the edges of her fingers.

I lean forward and make an exaggerated chomping sound as I wrap my lips around the fork and slide the meat from the end, my eyes never leaving hers.

Zach cheers and stabs another piece, lifting it to my mouth. "Again!"

"Nope," I say, pressing my lips together tight. "Now I get to feed you."

I pierce a piece of chicken from his plate and lift it in front of him.

He eyes the food and mimics me, pressing his lips together before pointing at my plate. "Nope."

Shit.

I was really hoping he hadn't understood that part of the story and wants me to feed me from his plate, so I could at least save the ribs for later.

"Okay," I sing-song. Holding a silent funeral for my stomach and the ribs that are no longer mine, I cut a small piece and offer it to Zach.

He gives me the biggest smile and chomps down on the fork, rubbing his belly as he chews.

"Is that good?"

He nods and offers me the chicken once again.

We go back and forth until half the food is gone from both of our plates.

"Alright bud," I start, "I think it's time for you to show us all your skills."

"All skills," he mimics.

"Exactly." I stab a piece of my ribs and put it in my mouth, savoring the taste with an emphatic "Yum."

Zach looks down at his plate, then glances at mine.

"Now it's your turn."

The table goes quiet—everyone fully invested in my endeavor to get Zach to use a fork on his own.

He eyes our plates again, before he reaches over and stabs a piece of my ribs and brings it to his lips. He makes a big show with a chomping sound as he slides it from the fork into his mouth and gives a loud, "Yum."

The entire table erupts in cheers. Holt and Bash stand, circling their fists over their heads, and Enzo pats Zach on the back, telling him how awesome that was.

But it's Leigh who has my attention.

Her blue eyes are locked on Zach, the silver tears that rimmed her eyes before now fall freely as she clutches her sweater in a tight fist. She tries to blink them back, sucking in a sharp breath. Then another. Until her chest heaves and I realize it's not sadness she's holding back, but panic.

Shit.

I press my hands to the table and stand, which catches her attention.

As if she knows she's been caught, she quickly backs her chair up and stands, darting from the room.

"Enzo, you've got Zach," I say as I grab the jacket she left behind and follow my girl into the cold.

Chapter Twelve

LEIGH

The wind nips through the tiny holes in my sweater, and I instantly regret my decisions as I stumble across the deck to the railing.

But I can't go back in there.

My knuckles turn white as I grip the weathered wood, willing it to ground me in reality. I suck in another breath to force air into my lungs.

This is okay.

I'm okay.

I'm not losing him.

He's just spending time with Luca.

I wanted this.

For Zach.

He needs this.

It's just dinner.

But it's more than that.

This isn't a fucking play date.

This is real.

They are connecting. Making memories. They are forming a bond that rivals my own.

And that scares the living shit out of me.

Because what if Luca's not his father?

What happens when he leaves?

When his family doesn't want Zach because he's my son too. The thief of Shady Grove.

I suck in another ragged breath—and exhale.

Over and over between choked sobs.

My lungs burn, but no matter how hard I try, I don't feel like I'm getting enough air.

"Leigh."

The disembodied voice is faint over the pounding of my heart in my ears.

"Leighton."

Luca?

I want to turn around, but I can't.

I'm frozen.

Literally and figuratively.

Running out in my sweater and leggings, sans coat and gloves, was a terrible idea.

I just needed to get out of there.

I needed to breathe.

Oh, the irony that now I can't force a simple breath into my lungs.

"Fuck, you're already shivering."

Am I?

I'm fairly certain that's just my body freaking out right alongside my heart, which is doing double-time against my ribcage.

Am I having a heart attack?

Shit.

Is this me dying?

At least Zach will have Luca.

Maybe this was meant to happen?

No.

I can't die.

Not like this.

"You're not dying."

Did I say that out loud?

"Are you sure?" My voice is embarrassingly small.

Luca drapes my coat over my shoulders and presses his chest to my back, wrapping his coat around us both. Gently, he covers my hands with his and, one finger at a time, pries them from the railing. Once he's got them all detached, he spins me in his arms and pulls them to his lips, warming them with his breath.

"I promise."

And I think I believe him.

Maybe.

Then again, maybe he's in on it, and it's a way to get Zach all to himself.

God, my brain is a fucked-up place.

I tip my head back, still struggling to catch my breath.

My chest hurts. My brain hurts. My heart hurts.

Luca mutters a string of curses as he continues to blow hot air on my frigid fingers.

I want to tell him they aren't that cold and rip them from his grasp. He doesn't get to be nice to me. Not right now. Not when I don't know why my body is drawn to him when it absolutely shouldn't be. Not when I'm going to die, and he's going to leave and fuck everything up after being the perfect almost dad to Zach.

"Leigh, tell me what you see," he murmurs against my hands.

"What?" I gasp.

"Five things you see. Tell me."

"No."

"Five things," he growls, and my body goes still.

Seeing in his eyes that he's not going to let me have this moment without him fucking it up, I concede a half-hearted, "Fine."

Fucking moody, selfish, billionaire, asshole.

My eyes dart left, then right, searching for anything tangible before a stray thought sneaks in.

Is there a wrong answer here?

Can it be anything?

Shit. I don't know.

"Out of your head, Leigh. The first thing you see."

A wild hair, plastered to his forehead beneath his beanie, catches my eye.

My throat feels thick. Impossible to swallow, but I manage to squeak, "Hair."

"Good. That's one." He takes both my hands in one of his large palms and the other moves beneath my coat to the small of my back, keeping me anchored close to him.

My gaze trails down past his perfectly sculpted brows. "Eyes."

His breath warms my hands. "That's two."

He traces tiny, even-pressured circles with his fingers against my shirt. "What color are they?"

"Blue."

And what a beautiful shade of blue they are. Like an iceberg that flipped over, seeing the sun for the first time. They sparkle.

"Good. What else do you see?"

My gaze slips lower. "Lips."

His tongue darts out and wets the soft pink pillows—masculine yet still far too pretty for a man. "That's three. Something else."

Lower, I latch on to the sliver of silver skin at the base of his throat. "Scar."

His brow furrows. "Huh?"

"Right here." I tug a hand free and trace the puckered skin.

Luca shivers and swallows hard before shifting slightly back. "Uh, good." His voice wobbles. "Two more things."

I want to ask how he got it, but that's too much for my brain to handle. Instead, I keep to his directions, following the hollow of his neck back up to his jaw—which, unlike this morning, is now shadowed with hair.

"Scruff."

"Do you like it?" he whispers.

I dip my head toward him and murmur. "It suits you."

It makes him look like a rugged book boyfriend. The kind that use their scruff to tickle your thighs. Especially up here in the mountains. All he needs is a flannel instead of his bougie designer jacket.

Mouth moving faster than my mind, I blurt out, "It makes you look less like an uptight prick."

Shit. Why did I say that?

Heat fills my cheeks, and I press my forehead to my lifted forearms as if that will make me shrink and disappear.

"Noted." Luca's chest rumbles with a chuckle and his hand tightens on my back, pulling me closer to him. "One more thing, Little Thief."

"Hands." I wiggle mine in front of him. "Thank you for warming them."

"You're welcome." He gives them a gentle squeeze and releases them. "Now I want you to let me see those beautiful blue eyes of yours and take four deep breaths with me."

Pulling from whatever manic bravery I have left, I tip my head back. His eyes connect with mine, and I'm surprised there isn't an ounce of pity, only encouragement.

"In through your nose, out through your mouth."

I accept his instructions, and latching on to his life-giving gaze, he becomes the roots that ground me.

With each slow breath, my chest loosens. The weight of my worries lifts. The panic morphs into safety. Until finally I'm able to fill my lungs completely.

"Good," Luca coos, a steadfast reassurance.

Feeling a little more settled and a lot less like I'm going to pass out, I step back and take control of my hands. I slip them through the sleeves of my coat, wrapping myself in a hug. It's nowhere near as soothing as Luca's embrace, but it gives me the space to recalibrate and remember where I am.

Luca's eyes never leave me. He watches me like a hawk. He waits with infinite patience until I give him an appreciative nod.

"Do you want to talk about it?"

A wince of dread flickers over my face. "If I say no, will you leave it alone?"

"All signs point to not a chance in hell," he says with the barest hint of a smirk.

I drop my shoulders in defeat, my gaze falling to the floor, and I wish it would open up and swallow me whole. This isn't how this trip was supposed to go.

None of it.

Not Luca and I fighting.

Not his friends welcoming me.

Not Zach having the time of his life with this new family.

I suck in a breath and hold it, staving off the panic that is all too willing to slither its way back in.

"Hey." He steps toward me and brings a finger to my chin, lifting it so I have no choice but to meet his gaze. "There's nothing to be ashamed of, but talking about what set it off can help."

My brow furrows. "Excuse me?"

"The panic attack."

"Is that what that was?" I consider my spiral and all the times Indie and I have helped Willow through her panic attacks. She's never said it felt like a heart attack. More like overwhelming racing thoughts. Which absolutely checks out, but the rest? I've never experienced that before.

"Was it your first one?" His kindness shines through once again, and as much as I like it, I'm not sure what to do with it, or how long it will last before the pendulum swings the other way.

Why did it have to be *him* who followed me out here? Why couldn't it have been Bash or Holt? Hell, I'd even take Enzo at this point.

So I do what I do best. Protect my heart. Deflect. Distract.

"That was terrible." I force a halfhearted chuckle. "Remind me never to do *that* again."

"Then we should definitely talk about it." Luca steps back, giving me the space I need and gestures toward the small seating area against the cabin sheltered away from the wind.

He watches as I hesitate and sighs. "Leigh. I'm not the bad guy."

I snort. "I'm pretty sure you are the very definition of the bad guy in my book."

He flinches like I've slapped him. "I deserve that."

"You deserve more."

"I do." He nods, having the decency to look remorseful. "But please. This isn't about you and me right now. It's just about you. I'll even sign one of your fancy NDAs that doesn't allow me to speak of this moment ever again."

I roll my eyes, but ultimately follow and slide up next to him on the small bench.

We sit in silence for a beat, nothing but the wind and rustle of the trees between us. I relax back against the cabin, my body feeling as though I just ran a damn marathon.

Luca is the first to break the silence. "Jack used to have panic attacks."

"He did?" I perk up at this bit of information. Each of the guys holds Jack's memory close to their chest, never wanting to give too much information without the others present. Luca sharing this with me shows a level of trust I wasn't expecting.

Luca nods and leans back, his head resting against the cabin. "Yeah. He was adopted and from a young age had a rough relationship with his brother because their parents doted on him due to his first battle with his illness. The problem is, he also had a huge heart, which caused him to panic when everyone wasn't getting along."

Heart in my throat, I softly ask, "What did he have?"

"Cancer."

"I'm sorry."

Fuck, I hate those words. They change nothing. Jack is still gone. His friends still grieve him. His family is still brokenhearted. Which is only confirmed by Luca's weak answer.

"Me too."

The silence stretching between us could fill an ocean. It's rough. Unbearable. And Luca brought it upon himself to help make me feel better.

Nope.

That's a thought to examine later. Alone. When I can't be distracted by the way his lower lip juts out and worries ever so slightly when he's feeling vulnerable.

But maybe this olive branch is exactly what we need. Luca wanted a fresh start, and while I'm not sure I can forget the past, I need to know who it is my son may or may not be spending Christmas with for years to come. I need to know who Luca Donati is now.

"How did you all meet?"

An endearing smile splits his lips. "Freshman year of college, we were all suite mates in the freshman athletics dorms."

"That must have been a fun suite." If they were anything like Indie, Willow, and me at boarding school, it was probably also a lot of trouble.

"We hated each other. Well, all of us, except Jack, hated each other. There isn't a world where that much testosterone should be put together."

"But you all played team sports?"

"Golf is not a team sport."

A small giggle escapes me. "Okay, most of you."

"Right, but we all played different sports. Which led to arguments about which was better."

"Fucking men." I roll my eyes, but mostly I'm impressed. It's all so normal. Wholesome even. And between Bash's stories this morning and this, I'm beginning to see a different side to Luca. One that isn't pretentious or selfish.

"You aren't wrong."

"So what happened?" I ask, invested in their story. "What brought you all together?"

"Believe it or not, our first Christmas."

"Really?" I tease, not believing it for a second. "That sounds like something out of a Hallmark movie."

"Those were always Jack's favorite. I can't count the number of times I came home and caught him crying on the couch." He chuckles and blinks away his own glassy tears threatening to fall. "That first Christmas Enzo and I weren't going home because of…" He hesitates for a beat but keeps going. "Well, that's a story for another time—but Bash and Holt were in season, so they were around, and Jack stayed behind because he insisted that's what friends did."

"He sounds like a smart guy." I turn up the corners of my mouth to hide the wave of emotion that hits me. I'll never get to meet this man who managed to get this ragtag group of guys on the same page.

"The smartest," Luca agrees. "Jack waited until we were all out of the suite, and when we came back, it looked like Christmas had thrown up on every available surface. He claimed it was because Christmas was his favorite holiday, but I think he knew it was exactly what we needed. Enzo and I were in the thick of family drama, Bash was homesick, and Holt had just gone through a bad breakup."

I file away the tiny bit of information about his family with a mental note to ask about it later. "And what happened?"

"We all got super drunk on hot chocolate and peppermint schnapps and fell asleep on the couches. From that moment on, we were inseparable."

"So basically all it took to get through to you guys was a good old-fashioned sleepover?"

Luca tips his head back and laughs. Like really laughs. It's deep and rich. He clutches his stomach, and I'm almost certain there are tears in his eyes.

And I'm lost in the sight of him. He might be an asshole one moment and sweet the next, but I don't think I've ever seen him look so carefree.

It's beautiful.

Devastatingly so.

I look away as he catches his breath, needing a moment of my own.

"When did you guys find out he was sick?" I whisper, and the way he drops his chin to his chest and sighs, I almost kick myself for asking.

But I need to know.

I need to understand. After everything Holt and Bash shared, I'm convinced so much of who Luca is now is wrapped in this story—this moment of his life.

"Senior year." Luca pauses and scrubs his hand down his face. "He had been losing weight and went to the doctors only to find out the cancer had returned. It was so far along that there wasn't anything they could do. He was gone in a matter of weeks."

"Oh my God," I breathe and, without thinking, reach over and take his hand in mine. Giving it a gentle squeeze, I channel every healing vibe I have left in my body. "I am so sorry, Luca."

He returns my squeeze, and a half smile tips his lips. "Me too. But I'm so glad I got the chance to have him in my life. Without him, I wouldn't be here. With the guys. Or with you."

My head tilts in question. "With me?"

He nods. "I was only at the fundraiser the night we conceived Zach because that's the hospice company that took care of Jack."

"Oh." I use my free hand to tug my coat tighter against the cold, ignoring how my stomach flutters at the way he's making it sound like we were destined to be there that night. "I always wondered why you were there. It didn't seem like your kind of event."

Indie would say it's fate.

Willow, serendipitous luck.

Me? I'm firmly in the camp of everything happens for a reason, but fate and destiny are bullshit.

Luca continues. "We rotate who goes each year. Most of the time, though, it's Enzo, Bash, or me, since Holt still has games to attend."

"But aren't Bash and Holt's teams in season right now?"

"Yeah, but Christmas is sacred." The whimsy in his voice is downright adorable. The way these grown ass men covet this holiday has me almost believing in its magic again.

Almost.

"What about when you were playing?" It's the only aspect of Bucket List Christmas I didn't get the chance to ask Bash and Holt about.

"We all had it written into our contracts that we'd be missing those games."

"Awww," I sing-song, clutching his hand to my chest. "That is the sweetest, most thoughtful thing I've ever heard."

"We try," he says, taking a mock bow.

I blink up at him. "You're not what I expected."

"I tried to tell you that."

He did. Over and over. During spring training. In countless messages. On the phone. And since we've been here.

And yet I'm still surprised every time he proves me wrong.

But maybe it's time I meet him halfway.

I inhale a deep, steadying breath. Exhaling slowly, I admit, "I got scared inside."

Luca straightens—his gaze going hard. "Why? Did one of the guys say something?"

"No, they're great," I reassure him, trying to find the right words. "It was you and Zach. I—It's always just been the two of us. Me and him against the world. Seeing you guys together, it—If you're his father, this is the start of something new for him that doesn't include me. And as his mom, that's terrifying."

He searches my face and confusion pleats his brows. "I'm not here to exclude you or replace you, Leigh."

"Logically I know that but tell that to my mom brain."

He lifts a brow. "Mom brain?"

"Listen," I admonish. "It's a real thing. Just wait until you're so in love with that little boy that you will literally rip your own heart from your chest if it means saving him."

Luca drops my hand and throws his up in mock surrender. "I believe you."

I once again search his face for any malice and raise a brow when I still find none. Even when he's been angry, it's always been because of hurt or defeat, but never maliciousness.

"I'm struggling with reconciling the man in front of me from the man who stood in front of our town and lied."

"I know. And I'm—"

"Please, let me finish."

He snaps his mouth shut and nods, threading his fingers through mine once more, giving a gentle squeeze.

I don't pull away even though I should. A part of me likes the weight of his presence, ensuring me that he's there and he's listening.

As much as I needed his story, he needs to hear mine.

"You told the entire town I was a thief. They ostracized me, and that broke me. Then when they asked you again, you doubled down and said our house should be searched to make sure I didn't steal from anyone else. And because you're a Donati, they listened. Not that they found anything, but the damage had been done. Every summer until I left for college, I was alone with only my mom and dad to talk to because no one wanted to associate with the town thief. My family lost clients and their business struggled to stay afloat until my parents died."

His hand tightens around mine, but he doesn't utter a word, allowing me the space to continue.

"I thought that was the worst of it until my grandparents tried to earn their way back into the good graces of the Shady Grove elite by having your mother arrange a match for me. But really, it was so they could gain access to the trust fund my parents left to me. Only I can't access it until I'm thirty or get married. Thankfully, I got pregnant, and your mother wouldn't dare sully anyone's name with a bastard child. So really, I guess I should be thanking you."

"I—" Luca looks away, and his voice trembles. "I didn't know."

I let out a frustrated scoff. "How could you? You were off at college making friends, celebrating Christmas, and working your way to the big show."

"Leigh, I—"

"I know you're sorry." My words catch on a sob. "I know you didn't know. But as I said before, those are just words, Luca. This is my life, not some game."

"I know." His voice trembles, and then becomes a little steadier. "I know. And I promise if it takes till my last breath, I'll make it up to you."

I shake my head, and even though I don't want to cry in front of him again over this, a traitorous tear falls down my cheek. "It's not about me anymore. I'm a big girl. It's about that little boy in there. If he's yours, don't fail him."

Luca reaches up and catches the tear with his thumb. "I won't." It's a solemn promise. Full stop. Do not pass go. He means it.

And I want to believe him.

But Luca isn't done.

He tightens his grip on my cheek and pierces my soul with his candor. "But what if I want it to be about you too? What if I don't want to fail you either?"

My jaw drops.

Me?

He wants it to be about me?

What does that even mean?

I'm saved from asking or answering when Zach comes running up and wraps his arms around me, followed closely by Bash, Enzo and Holt walking out of the cabin.

"You guys ready for a toast with the shittiest beer on the planet?" Bash asks, holding up the five cans of Coors Light cradled in his arms.

Enzo scrunches his nose and grabs a can from the pile. "I still don't understand how Jack loved this stuff."

"Listen," Holt reasons, grabbing a can for himself. "The bucket list said drink a beer in the Coors mountains." He lifts the can, lining up the iconic blue ridges with their real-life counterparts. "So here we are."

"Looks like duty calls," I say to Luca, nodding to the pile.

I turn, discreetly wiping my face so none of the guys see just what a mess I am when Bash chimes in, "Oh no, one of these is for you, baby momma."

"No, this is your thing." I backpedal, picking up Zach and heading for the cabin. "I wouldn't want to intrude."

Holt smirks and offers me a can. "Come on, Leigh. Jack would have wanted you to."

"And now that you know how we all met, and how Bucket List Christmas came to be, you can't say no," Luca adds.

"I—"

"Just give in, Leigh," Enzo pipes up. "They aren't going to let you out of it."

I sigh playfully. "Fine. Give me the damn beer."

The guys all cheer, and secretly I'm happy to be toasting to the man who brought them together. What they have is something so few get to cherish, let alone witness. It makes me miss Indie and Willow even more. Our sisterhood of the traveling smut is the equivalent of their bucket list boys.

"Anyone care to make this interesting?" Bash wiggles his eyebrows with an impish smile.

Holt doesn't miss a beat and pulls out a set of keys from his pocket. "Shotgun race?"

"Last one to finish has to wear *the* costume while we decorate the tree tonight."

"Deal," Holt says, and the two of them glance around to the group.

"Ugh. Fine." Enzo pulls a pen from his jacket.

Key's in hand, Luca chimes in, "You know I won't turn down a challenge."

They all swivel their heads to me.

Luca cocks a goading brow. "Leigh?"

I set Zach down and stand up, joining their circle. "Someone give me a key to use."

The guys each let out a whoop or cheer, and Zach joins them as Luca works a key off his ring.

"Don't lose that."

"Why? What's it the key to?"

"My heart," he simpers.

I roll my eyes. "Does that line actually work?"

"Unfortunately, yes," Enzo confirms. "Thank goodness you're too smart for that."

"I always knew you were my favorite twin."

"Watch it, Little Thief." Luca points a glare in my direction, but it's paired with a smile that tells me I'll pay for it later.

Bring it on, sweetheart.

"On that note." Holt lifts his beer to the center of the circle. "To Jack—the best of us. Gone too soon."

I look around the group, committing to memory the solemn smiles each of the guys wears and the sorrow in their eyes. It's a haunting kind of love and loss that's beautiful in its own right. It's a shared moment I will cherish forever. No matter how this plays out.

"To Jack."

Chapter Thirteen

LUCA

I'm going to kill Bash.

He knew what he was doing when he made that wager. Of course, there was no way he could have known Zach would wrap his tiny arms around my leg the moment we started chugging, melting my heart into a damn puddle. Any sane person would have taken the loss and savored the moment.

Which is exactly what I did. And while I don't regret it, or the giggle that came from Zach when I picked him up and spun him around, I'm absolutely suffering the consequences of my actions.

As if I didn't already look ridiculous in these red and white striped tights and fur lined, velvet red shorts, adding the shirt with the bells hanging from the collar and sleeves really amps up the absurdity. Maybe if it fit right, the outfit would be fine, but at two sizes too small, it's not giving Santa's helper as much as it's giving male stripper on Christmas Eve.

Never let it be said Luca Donati doesn't pay his debts like a damn gentleman.

Throwing the shirt aside, I spin around in front of the mirror in my room and do a bend test. First, to make sure the tights won't rip when stretched around my thick thighs, but also to double-check my balls aren't about to fall out the back of these damn shorts.

I'm face down, ass up when a giggle that is far too high pitched to belong to one of the guys meets my ears.

"That's some outfit you got there."

At least it's not the string bikini this time. Then she'd really be getting a show.

I crane my neck and look over my shoulder to where Leigh stands in the doorway. She's changed out of her snow gear and into a pair of cozy looking black leggings with an oversized sweater that drapes off her shoulder, exposing her collar bone.

It isn't a part of a woman that I previously would have considered sexy, but on Leigh it might as well be an ankle in the eighteen hundreds because my dick is registering it as scandalous.

"You checking out my ass, Little Thief?"

"I—" Pink fills her cheeks, and her eyes drop to my ass then snap up, like she couldn't help herself. "No."

I chuckle. She's flustered, and it's freakin' adorable.

As I straighten and face her, Leigh freezes—her body once again betraying her. Those curious blue eyes examine the bare skin of my chest, lingering on their way down until she reaches the bulge in my shorts.

"Did you need something?" I intend for it to sound nonchalant, but it comes out sounding husky and provocative.

It's her fault for staring at my dick.

"Your nipples are pierced," she blurts out, and I get the feeling she meant for it to be an inside thought.

My eyes track to the barbells and back up at her. "So they are. I didn't know we were doing bodily inspections. Does this mean I get a turn too?"

Her mouth gapes like a cute little fish out of water before she gets a grasp on the moment. "In your dreams, Donati."

God damn.

Usually, I hate my last name and everything it's attached to, but when it rolls off Leigh's tongue, somewhere between a flirt and a curse, I think it might have just unlocked a new kink.

"Every night, baby," I purr.

That earns me one of her charming little eye rolls. "Bash sent me to ask if you were ready for your grand entrance."

"Is Zach done with his bath?"

"He's clean and ready for bed," she confirms with a nod.

The little stinker was a handful after dinner, not wanting to get ready for bed. It wasn't until I promised he could help me decorate the tree that he eagerly followed Leigh to the guesthouse.

I hated watching them go, and almost fought her for the right to be the one to handle his nighttime routine, but by the time we got home from the mountain, it was clear Leigh was still on edge and needed the time with him more than I needed to make new memories with him.

I do a once over, happy to see she's got a bit more color in her face and no longer has a problem meeting my gaze.

Except for when she gets caught starting.

She scans the rest of the bedroom, and I'm keen to let her. I want her to know me. They linger on my nightstand where there's a copy of *You Will Rock as a Dad*.

"It's just a little light bedtime reading. Thought I should be prepared."

Leigh pops her shoulders and grins. "I prefer smut, but whatever floats your boat."

I clutch the imaginary pearls at my throat.

Leigh giggles.

She *giggles*.

It's an intoxicating sound. One I wish I could bottle and keep—to get me through every moment that feels hopeless.

"Why am I not surprised you read your porn like a noblewoman?"

"Because you know I have impeccable taste."

That she does.

She also has all the layers of an onion but with the poise of a viscountess. Keeping her thoughts close to chest, only letting things like this slip when she's comfortable. The same way she did earlier today when she admitted she's scared I'm taking Zach from her.

The panic in her eyes scared the shit out of me. But learning about the ripple effects my actions have had on her life nearly broke me.

I'm damn lucky she's standing here at all.

The image of her sitting on that bench, tears in her eyes, is something I will never forget or forgive myself for.

Fuck, just thinking about it makes my chest hurt.

There's no way I could've known. I was young and dumb with a misconstrued idea of right from wrong.

I should've found her sooner. Protected her from my mother. I should've admitted the lies I told and saved her from the fallout.

Should've.

Could've.

Didn't.

But I'm going to fix it. I'm going to—shit, I don't know, but I am going to prove I'm worthy of her and Zach.

"Luca?"

"Huh?" I look up from the spot on the floor I've been boring a hole into while making silent vows to myself.

"You ready?"

"Oh. Yeah." I grab the jingle shirt from the bed and slip it over my head, silently living for the way Leigh tries to hide she's watching my skin disappear from view.

She's going to need to knock that shit off if she wants me to continue keeping my hands to myself.

I offer her my arm as I meet her at the door. "Ready to rock around the Christmas tree?"

Her lips press into a line, and she shakes her head. And I remember I still need to ask her why she hates my favorite holiday.

Later.

Because, when she slips her hand around my arm and grips it tight, I forget about anything else.

I like having her there.

I want her there more.

"You missed a spot near the bottom," Bash hollers from the opposite side of the room. He's cutting pieces of printer paper into snowflakes—and I might be mistaken from this distance—but I'm fairly certain he's making all the cutouts dick-shaped. You'd never know the guy was a star-defensive-lineman-turned-team-owner with the way he acts like a frat boy ninety percent of the time.

Not that I have much room to talk in this outfit. I tug at the crotch of the tiny red shorts in an attempt to lengthen them, but it's no use.

Might as well make the best of an embarrassing situation.

I round the tree and bend over, making a show in front of the guys. They hoot and holler as I adjust the lights that really didn't need adjusting in the first place.

Zach, who has taken up a spot at the bottom of the tree with the sole goal of making sure my string of lights gets as tangled as possible, watches me move my ass back and forth.

A large toothy grin stretches across his small face, and he pops up beside me and bends over, shaking his little diaper butt alongside mine.

The guys cheer him on, and he giggles like it's the funniest thing he's ever done.

It's just another reason I love them. This is my life now and aside from giving me shit for not telling them, they jumped in with both feet and accepted it.

In my periphery, I peek at Leigh sitting curled on the couch, worried that another moment like this might be too much for her. I fully expect her to be watching her son's first twerking experience, but instead her eyes are locked on me.

Interesting.

I lift a hand and wiggle my fingers at her, letting her know she's been caught.

Of course, she snaps her gaze back to the game on the TV, but that doesn't stop the pretty pink hue tinting her cheeks or the knowing smile that tips her lips.

It's right then, I decide to make it my life's mission to keep it there. I want her smiling and giggling every day, because that woman deserves every ounce of happiness.

And maybe a dash of sexy embarrassment too.

The night continues on in a blissful blur.

Zach continues to "help" me decorate the tree while Leigh snuggles on the couch between Bash and Enzo as they watch Holt's team attempt a Hail Mary comeback in the third period. The way she curls up with her knees to her chest and takes the spiked hot chocolate Bash offers, she looks like she belongs there. Like we've all been friends for years. You'd never know she just met them, or that she hates me.

The game ends with Holt's team winning in overtime, which only serves to bolster the mood in the room. Bash and Enzo drunkenly dance around as they hang the dick snowflakes around the room, changing the lyrics from a popular Christmas song to *walkin' round in women's underwear.* Holt hangs the stockings over the fireplace, adding the two I ordered from a store in town for Zach and Leigh.

Still curled on the couch with a lazy smile, Leigh's eyes bounce between the guys and Zack, who is playing with the bucket of tinsel and ornaments at my feet.

"Hey Baby Momma, why don't you help Holt and I hang this mistletoe?"

"Bash," I growl, knowing damn well he's asking to get a rise out of me.

Leigh offers him an all too sweet smile. "As fun as it sounds to be sandwiched between the two of you under the mistletoe, Christmas isn't really my thing. I'm happy to supervise, though."

"What?" Holt and Bash gasp at the same time.

"Why's that?" Enzo asks, and I step out from behind the tree, pinning a glare in his direction.

Leigh's gaze lands on me, and I reassure her. "You don't have to tell us anything,"

"No, it's fine," she says, but the way she twists her hands in her lap reveals just how uncomfortable she is. "It's because Christmas was my parents' favorite holiday. After they died, it sort of just lost the magic for me. I've been trying to find it again for Zach's sake, but it's been difficult."

Fuck.

And here I've been shoving the holiday down her throat.

A chorus of "shits" and "I'm sorrys" echo from my friends, but all I can do is watch my girl.

She smiles and I watch as she does the same thing she did today after her panic attack. She pushes the feelings deep down for the sake of those around her.

"This is actually the first time I've enjoyed holiday festivities," she admits, bringing joy back into the equation.

Bash crosses the room and plops down next to her on the couch, draping an arm over her shoulder. "Bucket List Christmas has that effect on people."

"I'd like to say it's us," Holt adds, "but Jack created something special that first Christmas."

"It's infectious," Enzo chimes in.

"It really is." She gives a cursory glance around the room, stopping on Bash, then Enzo, and Holt. Finally, she ends with heartfelt eyes on me. "Thank you for letting me be a part of it."

My heart races hard and steady against my chest.

She's thanking me.

Not my friends.

Me.

I can't look away—dumbfounded by what the hell this small gesture means.

Of course, Bash has to go and ruin it.

"Anytime, Baby Momma."

Leigh breaks our connection, shaking her head at the nickname she's never going to live down.

"Speaking of babies, it looks like mine is officially done."

All four of us swing our gaze to look at where Zack has curled up under the tree, cuddling his stuffed horse and a pile of ornaments like they are his precious treasures.

"I should get him to bed." Leigh swings her legs out and sets her mug on the coffee table.

"Let me," I offer.

She opens her mouth to protest but stops herself. Pressing her lips together to hold back whatever smart comment tips her tongue, she nods.

I carefully scoop up the sleeping toddler, loving the way he snuggles into my chest. He's adorable when he's awake, but sleeping in my arms, he's damn near angelic.

Leigh follows as I head out of the living room. Instead of turning toward the door that leads to the guesthouse, I head deeper into the house.

"Where are you going?" Leigh whispers.

"If you don't mind, we have an extra room. That way, we don't have to take him out in the cold, and you can hang out for a bit longer."

I fully expect her to say no. But I wanted her to know this isn't just about Zach. Not anymore. If I'm honest, it never was. As much as I want him here, I want her here too.

Her nose wrinkles, and she contemplates my offer.

When we get to the room across the hall from my own, I motion for her to open the door for me.

Leigh's jaw drops when she walks in. Four bunk beds with full-size bottom mattresses line the two walls, and a crib that has been converted to a toddler bed sits below the window.

She follows as I tuck Zach into the small bed and lean down to press a kiss to his forehead. I freeze mid kiss, realizing this isn't something I've done until now. It just felt right.

Of course, now I'm second-guessing if it was the right thing to do in front of Leigh.

When I turn around, she's staring inquisitively and chewing her lip like she's holding back from saying something.

I nod toward the door so we don't wake up Zach. Once we get into the hallway, she leans against the wall and looks up expectantly.

"This was here the whole time?" she whispers, nodding back toward the closed door.

"You wanted your own space," I start, pleading my case. "I didn't want you to feel obligated or like I manipulated you into staying in the main house after I—"

"Basically blackmailed me into being here, even though you had all the work already done?"

Fuck. I let out an exasperated breath and run a frustrated hand through my hair. "Yeah, that."

I wait for her to continue berating me, ready to take whatever it is she gives, but instead, her voice softens and a weak, "Thank you" slides out.

I do a double take, blinking slowly to make sure I heard her right.

It's the second time she's thanked me tonight.

And God, the things it's doing to me.

Having her thanks is a form of praise I didn't know I needed.

"I'm not saying I'm okay with what you did, but I appreciate you respecting my wishes."

"I—well shit—" I stammer. "That isn't what I was expecting you to say."

Her eyes sparkle in the dimly lit hallway and it takes everything in me not to close the distance between us so I can really see their beauty. Or maybe I just want to be close to her. I definitely shouldn't. And not only because I'm in this fucking elf costume that is doing next to nothing to hide the blood diverting its way to my dick.

Her tongue darts out and wets her pillowy lips, and I desperately want to know if they are as soft as they look.

Again, not helpful. Not when there is still so much left unsaid between us.

"Leigh, I—"

"We should get back," she cuts me off.

I tilt my head in agreement, but as soon as she turns, I know I can't let the moment pass without saying something.

My hand darts out and wraps around her wrist. "Let me just ask you one thing."

She glances down at my hand and then up at me, giving a barely perceptible nod of her head.

"Go to dinner with me," I blurt out like the words might physically burn me if I don't say them.

"That's not a question."

"Share a meal with me," I clarify, again not asking. Afraid that if I give her more of a choice, she'll outright say no.

She shrugs my hand away, and her eyes find the ground between us. "I heard you. I'm just not sure that's the best idea."

"Take a chance. Get to know me. Let me get to know you. Neither of us is who we were ten years ago. And I think we both can admit that there's something between us, even if it's just the need to be the best co-parents we can possibly be to Zach."

She sucks her lower lip between her teeth. Something she does when she's taking the time to consider her opinion.

"Dinner only."

My heart dances in my chest. This is it. This is how we move forward. Just the two of us. We have to be us before we can be parents.

"Dinner only." I hold up three fingers. "Scout's honor."

Leigh huffs a laugh. "Like you were ever a Boy Scout."

"Guess you'll have to find out when we go to dinner tomorrow night," I counter with a playful wink.

She shakes her head, a yawn wracking her small form. "Is it okay if I just stay in the room with Zach tonight? I'd feel safer being in the house with him."

It's on the tip of my tongue to say she could sleep in my room, but I've already pushed as far as I dare for one night.

"Of course."

She turns to the door, her hand on the knob, when I stop her again. "Oh, and Leigh?"

"Hmm?"

And because I can't stop myself, I take a step forward, my chest touching her shoulder and pressing her into the door. I lower my head and brush the shell of her ear with my lips, ensuring she hears the vow I intend to make.

"I'm promising dinner, because more than anything, I want to know you. I want to grovel and get on my knees for you. I'll do whatever it takes to make you see I want this family. So. Fucking. Much." A shiver shakes her body, and she leans into me for support. Which I'm all too happy to provide. "I'm not going anywhere. And I need the record to show that even if Zach isn't mine, I still want you both. We can set whatever pace you want, but I don't want to only hate fuck you in vending machine closets. I want to fuck you for real. In my bed. Where we don't have to worry how loud you scream my name."

Her jaw drops, and she's rendered speechless.

I fucking love it.

My only hope is she was ready to hear my plea.

"Think about it," I whisper and press my lips to her bare shoulder. "I'll see you tomorrow, Little Thief."

Chapter Fourteen

LEIGH: I'm pretty sure I agreed to go out with Luca.

INDIE: Fuck yes.

WILLOW: Like on a date?

LEIGH: It's not a date.

LEIGH: But he did say he wants to fuck me.

INDIE: Wait what?! WHY DIDN'T YOU LEAD WITH THAT?!

LEIGH: Because I'm still freaking out.

LEIGH: I thought I'd wake up, and I don't know, not be still freaking out. Now I have to go spend the whole day with him doing cute Christmas shit and pretend I'm not spiraling about this damn dinner.

INDIE: THIS HAPPENED LAST NIGHT AND YOU'RE JUST TELLING US NOW?!

LEIGH: Focus Indie. What do I do?

INDIE: If the answer isn't obvious, I think we have a bigger problem.

LEIGH: INDIE.

WILLOW: Do you not want to sleep with him?

LEIGH: Me, a woman who hasn't been laid in over two years? Yes. Me, Zach's mom? Not so much. It seems too messy if he's the father.

WILLOW: Still no word on the paternity test?

LEIGH: He only sent it off yesterday. He's rich but not that rich.

INDIE: Do you want him to be Zach's dad?

LEIGH: No.

LEIGH: Yes.

LEIGH: I don't know. He's really good with Zach, and he's done his best to mostly respect my boundaries. He's committed to co-parenting. And his friends are amazing. Basically, on paper he's perfect.

WILLOW: But…

LEIGH: He's still a Donati.

WILLOW: Did he tell you the whole story?

LEIGH: No. But why do I get the feeling he told you?

WILLOW: I might have demanded he explain himself when he asked how to prepare for Zach.

LEIGH: AND YOU DIDN'T TELL ME.

INDIE: She wouldn't tell me either.

WILLOW: It's not my story to tell.

LEIGH: Bash said the same thing.

WILLOW: Go to dinner. Let him explain. If you still hate him afterwards, then don't fuck him.

LEIGH: I never said it was dinner.

WILLOW: ………

LEIGH: Are you talking to him?!

WILLOW: Gotta go. Bishop's mom is insisting I participate in some Lawson family tradition that involves a pickle.

INDIE: Yeah you're definitely going to have to explain that one later. Pickles and Christmas sound fun.

INDIE: As for you, Leigh, for what it's worth, he seems like he's trying. But I'm also just saying you don't have to love him to fuck him. You don't even have to like him.

LEIGH: Isn't that what got us here in the first place?

INDIE: Just don't get knocked up this time.

LEIGH: << middle finger emoji>>

INDIE: Don't do anything I wouldn't do.

LEIGH: That isn't saying much.

Chapter Fifteen

LEIGH: And you had to go and ruin the moment.

LUCA: You're saying you don't think about that night?

LEIGH: Even if I do, a lady doesn't kiss and tell.

LUCA: So you do think about it.

LUCA: What's your favorite part?

LUCA: Mine is a tie between you on your knees with my cock between those pretty little lips of yours, and you telling me exactly how you wanted me to fuck you.

LEIGH: LUCA!

LUCA: What? I already told you, Little Thief, I'm done pretending I don't want you in my bed.

LEIGH: Zach comes first, remember?

LUCA: No, you come first. Always.

LUCA: But if you must know, this is one hundred percent me thinking of Zach first. Not while you're coming, of course, but if we give this a shot then it's really what's best for him. He gets two parents who love him.

LEIGH: It's not that simple.

LUCA: It really is, but I know I've got more groveling and explaining to do. So you've got some time to consider my offer.

LEIGH: <eye roll emoji>

LEIGH: What's the plan for today? I need to know what to pack for Zach.

LUCA: How does Zach feel about Santa?

LEIGH: He likes the idea of him, but I think the beard freaks him out. Which is ironic, considering he's a social butterfly with everyone else.

LUCA: Noted. I'll make sure I shave.

LEIGH: You don't have to do that.

LUCA: Fine. I'll keep it short. I know you like the scruff.

LUCA: Ice skating?

LEIGH: A toddler on a hard surface and knives on our feet. Sounds fun.

LUCA: Okay, maybe next year on skating. Holt will be so disappointed.

LUCA: Ornament painting?

LEIGH: How long is the list of things you thought up for today's outing?

LUCA: Infinite.

LEIGH: Painting is fine.

LUCA: Christmas Market downtown?

LEIGH: Yes.

LUCA: Baking cookies?

LEIGH: No eating the cookie dough.

LUCA: Spoil Sport.

LUCA: Fine.

LEIGH: So plan for indoors and outdoors.

LUCA: Straight and to the point. Yes.

LEIGH: Okay we'll be ready in about twenty.

LUCA: Perfect.

LUCA: There's a travel mug of coffee on the island with your name on it.

LEIGH: Thank you.

LUCA: Damn. I like it when you do that.

LEIGH: What? Thank you?

LUCA: Yeah. Last night it made my dick hard too. Maybe I have a praise kink.

LEIGH: Want me to tell you you're a good boy?

LUCA: Maybe later. If you do that now, I'm going to have to take another shower or risk the guys seeing just how turned on I am.

LEIGH: But you're such a good fucking boy, thinking of me, making me my coffee. I'm a lucky girl.

LUCA: I hate you.

LEIGH: Enjoy your shower.

Chapter Sixteen

LEIGH

"Is everything okay in there?"

"Uhhh." The fear and uncertainty in Luca's voice is almost comical. "Yeah, I've got everything under control."

I'm not sure if he's trying to convince me or himself.

He was so confident when he told me he'd handle this diaper change. Because in his words, how hard could it be?

Which probably makes this all the more enjoyable. It's karmic retribution for all the blowout diapers I have changed alone over the last two years.

Still, it was incredibly sweet of him to handle one of the dirtier aspects of parenthood.

In fact, he's really stepped up today. He's handled everything from giggles, to meltdowns, to going with the flow and adjusting his carefully thought-out plan. Including when Zach didn't have the patience for the many layers of painting needed for ceramic ornaments.

Of course, Luca handled it by paying the shop's teenaged employee an extra couple hundred dollars to finish them for us. But who am I to judge when he has done everything to make today special for Zach?

And me.

You'd never guess Luca has only missed one Christmas with Zach from the way he crammed five years' worth of activities into one day. We've painted ornaments, caught snowflakes on our tongues, and sang Christmas carols at the top of our lungs (much to the dismay of passersby). At the town's small Christmas market, where Luca bought everything Zach touched to wrap and put under the tree, we sipped hot cocoa and laughed until our sides hurt. There was even a sweet moment Luca bought me a bracelet that had coffee cup charms because I did a double take while browsing. He had no idea it reminded me of my mom and our mornings together.

The magic of Telluride only made it more special. The small valley town is like something plucked from another time—every building is made of brick and every storefront has a purpose. There are restaurants, a post office, and a hardware store. Coffee shops, a bookstore, and a clothing boutique, each with lights sparkling in their windows to celebrate the upcoming holiday. There's no missing the sense of warmth radiating at every turn despite the frigid temperatures. People fill the sidewalks, but unlike in New York, where they walk with intent. Here, they stroll like they have nowhere to be except right here.

A loud cough that almost sounds like a gag pulls me from my dreamy thoughts, and I lean against the bathroom door.

"Is it supposed to be everywhere?" Luca asks, and seconds later I hear an actual heave. "And the smell. What died in this kid's ass?"

Pressing my lips together, I manage to stop my cackle, but there's no mistaking the humor in my tone. "Let me in."

"No, I got this."

I press my palm against the door, like he'll feel my encouragement through the wood. "Are you sure?"

There's a delay in Luca's answer, leaving me seconds away from going to the register of the small coffee shop to ask for a second key.

"Yeah. I'm almost done." There's another faint gagging sound, followed by Zach's faint giggles.

Three tense minutes pass before the handle to the bathroom jiggles, and Luca appears with Zach in his arms.

I expect shock and horror to be etched on his face, but both my boys are all smiles.

My stomach flips, then tightens.

Nope. Not my boys.

Geez. A single one-sided conversation with Luca about what he wants us to be and I'm already considering him mine. Don't get me wrong, it's all I've thought about all day. Him and me. Me and him. It's more complicated than a trigonometry equation. But every time his big blue eyes lingered just a fraction of a second too long in my direction, traitorous butterflies took flight in my stomach, and I definitely took notice.

Something has shifted between us in my mind, and I'm not sure I like it.

Maybe Indie was right, and I just need to fuck him.

It's not productive or a good idea, but maybe if I get him out of my system, I can think about everything objectively.

I swallow hard, forcing the thought from my mind. "All clean?"

"Yup." Luca pops the P at the end, as he lowers a squirming Zach to his feet.

"Hote?" Zach asks, pointing to where Holt and Enzo linger for a chance with the pretty redhead behind the counter, pretending to check out the selection of Christmas treats.

Freaking men.

In New York or Telluride, they're all the same.

"You can go to Holt," I say, watching as he quickly takes off and crosses the small shop. I wait until Holt has his hand and looks over at me, nodding a confirmation that he has him.

When I turn back, Luca's watching me with a glimmer of a smile.

"You trust my friends."

I tilt my head to the side, hiding the instant panic that grips my chest. "Should I not?"

"No, it's not that. I just—" He rakes a hand through his side-swept hair and squeezes the nape of his neck, a sheepish twinkle in his eyes. "It means a lot to me that you'd trust them. They're my family."

It takes me by surprise. Not only because he's right—I do trust them—but also because it's a slightly foreign concept for me. Sure, I trust my girls back home, and my neighbor Cynthia, who has become a surrogate grandmother to Zach. And then there are the guys on the Renegades. But those relationships took time and a lot of therapy on my part to foster. The Bucket List Boys—they came in like a wrecking ball. From the very moment I arrived, they demanded my attention. My trust. Over and over again, they've put my heart at ease, taking care of my son like he was already one of them. With them, it's just been…easy.

If only it could be that easy with Luca.

"They're good to Zach," I admit.

"And you," Luca adds the part I kept silent.

"And me," I echo.

Because they have been good to me. A silent force showing me, despite my reluctance, there are people out there outside the family I've created who can care about Zach and me.

I'm still reluctant to believe it's forever, but they've made cracks in my walls, and I fear I'll absolutely miss them when we're back in New York. Because even though they claim they aren't going anywhere, we are. Home.

Fuck.

Why does this all have to be so complicated?

"What's going on in that head of yours?" Luca asks as he reaches up and tucks a stray piece of hair behind my ear. His hand lingers on my cheek for a moment, his fingers rough. It's innocent but feels intimate, and

I restrain myself from leaning into his touch.

"I—" I pause, not ready to talk about the revelations of the day. So instead, before better sense takes hold, I blurt out the one thing we've yet to talk about. "What about your real family?"

He drops his hand, his face hardening into a scowl. "What about them?"

"Why are you here instead of there?"

There's been this kind of we-don't-talk-about-it aura from, not only Luca, but all the guys too. He's told me over and over he's not the guy he was before and made a few comments that make it sound like this is his only family, but none of it adds up. Christmas is for family, and I know damn well he's got one that didn't just let him go willingly. Even a Google search didn't give me any solid answers—believe me, I tried.

Luca's shoulders fall along with his gaze. For a long time, he contemplates what to say next until he finally looks up through his long lashes and sighs. "I don't want you to think I don't want to give you an answer. I do. I've owed you the explanation for months—years really—but can we put a pin in this until tonight? You deserve the whole story, and the apology you don't want me to give. I can't do that in the five minutes we have before either Zach comes looking for you, or Enzo and Holt need rescuing."

It's a fair request, but it doesn't stop the tense feeling that I might need all the answers before going out with him this evening. I should have let him talk yesterday at the cabin instead of insisting he hear my side of the story. It was petty, but I needed him to hear me. I needed him to understand I didn't need his words.

Only now I do.

How am I supposed to set the pace on whatever this is when I don't have all the facts?

While I can do casual with just about anyone else, there is nothing casual about what's brewing between me and Luca Donati.

I give a soft nod. "At dinner then."

"Thank you."

And because I can't help myself. I wink and whisper, "Good boy," as I walk away.

Luca groans and a swarm of drunk bees take flight low in my belly.

What the hell have I gotten myself into?

The rest of the day passes in a Hallmark Christmas blur. One where Luca and I don't cross paths unless we have to. There's always at least one of his friends between us, and any time we talk, it's short and uncharacteristically sweet. None of the guys say anything, but if their arched brows are anything to go on, they know something's off.

After finishing in town, we take the gondola back up to The Village so Zach can take a nap. I retreat to the guesthouse to get some work done.

Luca's detailed proposal for Monarch Hearts is spread out across the coffee table. I flip through the pages, reading every thoughtfully placed plan.

It's immaculate.

Incredible.

Honestly, I want to use his proposal as a template for every partnership moving forward. He took my ideas and expanded on them in a way that is not only efficient but allows for growth within the program to include more locations in each city, local events, and partnerships.

If I wasn't the current face of Renegade Hearts in New York so Willow can run the baseball team, I might ask if I could head up this branch, if only because I want to see how it all plays out.

In every detail, I can see Luca's unique thoughts. There's compassion and honesty. Loyalty and ambition. I see him—wearing his heart on his sleeve. The man who jumped in with both feet when he found out Zach might be his. The man who spends Christmas with his best friends, honoring the one they lost. The man who wants to get to know me so he can give my son the family he deserves.

And even though I am desperate to know the rest of the details that made him this way, I am smacked with a gut-wrenching truth.

It doesn't matter.

It doesn't. Fucking. Matter.

Of course, I still want to hear it. It's important for me to know, but this man is who he says he is now. Of all things, it took rifling through this damn proposal for me to see it, but what he said is true. We aren't the same people we were ten years ago, and the man he is today is a man I want to know.

I don't know how he did it, but that smooth-talking, obnoxious asshole wormed his way back into my life and heart.

There's still the question mark of what will happen if we find out he isn't Zach's father. But it would be a disservice to Zach, and myself, not to give him a chance.

Right?

My head spins, briefly unable to make sense of it all. There are still so many unknowns, and the need to protect the hearts of me and my son. But then I imagine what could be…

Holidays with the Bucket List boys.

Baseball games with Zach on Luca's shoulders.

Always having a date for stupid galas Willow doesn't want to attend.

Vending machine closets at said galas.

It's all there, in vivid detail, and for a split second, it doesn't seem so scary.

Chapter Seventeen

LUCA

I'm falling in love with this kid.

The way he scrunches his nose when he doesn't like something.

How he always wants to include everyone in what he's doing.

His sweet little voice as he tries to say my name.

I've got it bad.

Like ready to transplant my life to New York to be near him, bad.

Which terrifies me.

Because what happens if he's not mine?

How am I supposed to say goodbye after he's stolen a piece of my heart?

Not that I want to. I'm in this either way.

But Leigh is the wildcard.

After his nap, the guys and I kidnapped Zach so Leigh could have some time to herself and get ready for dinner without a toddler running around her ankles. He's been fed and watered, and now they are tackling dessert.

Or rather dessert is tackling them.

The kitchen is a disaster, but the warmth and laughter make it all worth it.

Zach giggles beside me and pushes his finger into the pile of flour on the kitchen island. He turns to me and slides it across my forehead, the same way Bash did to him.

"Imba." Zach giggles, copying the line from the *Lion King*, just like Bash.

I pull him against me in a hug, laughing along with him to hide the lingering fear beneath the surface.

It's only been a few days, but he already feels so ingrained into this tiny mismatched family.

Him and his mom.

And I could lose them both.

Physical pain manifests in my chest at the thought, and I reach up and rub the spot over the offending organ.

"Mama!" Zach yells, reaching his hands toward her as she walked through the mudroom door behind me.

I quickly lift him, so he doesn't fall from the chair, but also so he doesn't wrap his flour-covered-hands around Leigh.

Once I get Zach settled on my hip, I finally get the chance to look up. When I do, the first thing I notice is Holt, Bash, and Enzo frozen in place, jaws dropped.

Turning to see what has them all catching flies, my jaw falls right along with them.

She's dressed in *me*.

Leigh looked beautiful the night we reconnected at the hospice fundraiser.

And she was stunning when I saw her at the spring training gala.

But neither of those moments compares to seeing her now. She wears a little black dress, showing just enough cleavage that I'm liable to stare at her chest all night, paired with tights that are practically painted on, and knee-high boots which would look spectacular draped across my shoulders. But all that isn't what has my heart pounding and my dick twitching. No—she had to go and top it all off with a purple and white leather Monarchs bomber jacket with a gold number twenty-three stitched on the sleeve. My old number.

Mine.

Just like I want her to be.

Leigh's gaze darts between the four of us, standing there in stunned silence. "Uh—" She twists her hands together nervously across her stomach. "I hope you don't mind. I borrowed your jacket. Mine was still wet from the snow earlier."

Mind? She's lucky my friends and her son are in the room, otherwise she'd already be draped across the kitchen island so I could show her just how much I don't mind.

"Oh, he definitely doesn't mind," my twin mutters, hoisting Zach from my grip.

I glare daggers in his direction as I tug my apron off and step toward Leigh.

"It's fine," I manage, but what I really want to say is, *you can wear my clothes any time you want. What's mine is yours as long as it goes both ways.*

And by that, I mean everything under her clothes as well.

Not that I'm about to let her in on any of my less than chaste internal monologue.

I've already made my intentions known.

The ball is in Leigh's court now.

But damn, I hope when the night is over, she chooses to explore all those things.

She crosses the kitchen, stops in front of me, and leans down to kiss Zach's forehead. "These cookies look amazing."

Zach squirms in my arms, and I set him back down on his stool. The moment I do, he grabs a gingerbread cookie and offers it to Leigh. It's shaped like a star with way too much icing and sprinkles, but you'd never know it by the way her face lights up.

She takes a bite, and her exaggerated moan has me stifling a groan of my own.

"This is delicious," she croons, and Zach beams under her praise. "Did you make this?"

He nods confidently, and my heart melts even more.

"You did a great job," she tells him before looking up at the rest of us. "Thanks for keeping him occupied while I got ready."

The guys all answer at the same time.

"Of course."

"No problem."

"We love that kid."

Leigh's eyes soften, and I swear there's a hint of something more in her gaze, though I can't place it.

She turns back to Zach and leans down over the island so she's at his level. "You going to be good for these guys tonight?"

The toddler gives her an assertive nod before digging back into the flour in front of him.

Well, I'm glad he's confident, because I'm a ball of nerves.

I lift my head and narrow my gaze at my best friends. "You sure you're okay handling bedtime? We can be back before then if you need us to."

"Absolutely not," Holt reassures me as he returns to rolling out a mound of gingerbread dough. "I helped raise my sister. It's like riding a bike. We've got this."

"Plus"—Bash nods in Leigh's direction—"you need a night off as much as she does. You've been wound tighter than a damn tourniquet."

I groan and roll my eyes.

"On that note," Leigh says and offers me her hand, "I think it's time we go."

I stare at it, wondering if it's a trap. Outside of when I told her about Jack, she hasn't initiated any kind of contact with me.

Not to mention, I'm in awe of how okay she is with leaving him for the evening.

How did she manage to be away from him for an entire week during spring training? Or when she has to travel for Renegade Hearts? I've only known Zach for a few days, and I can't imagine missing a single moment of his life. What if something happens, and he needs us?

My eyes dart between her hand and Zach. "Okay, but you have our phone numbers if you need us."

"Yes, helicopter-dad." Enzo helps Zach back onto his chair, where he's already picking out the next cookie cutter he wants to use. "Now go. Leigh looks too beautiful to let this night off go to waste."

I glare daggers at my twin for the second time, silently reprimanding him for stealing my line.

He shrugs as if to say, *you should have said it first then.*

I hesitate, chewing the inside of my cheek before looking nervously in Leigh's direction. Her blue eyes unravel mine, and it's enough to spur me into placing my hand in hers.

We need this to figure out whatever the hell this thing between us is before I combust.

Turning, I raise one brow and gesture toward the door. "Shall we?"

Chapter Eighteen

LEIGH

We follow the petite redheaded hostess to a table overlooking the main downtown strip of Telluride. With the white tablecloths, candles and wine on the table, and twinkling lights outside—it's damn romantic.

I hate it.

Not because I don't love a top-notch romantic moment, but this isn't what I had in mind. It feels forced.

If Luca is trying to prove to me he's not the same guy I remember, he has a funny way of showing it by taking me to the kind of restaurant his parents would eat at.

Then again, how's he supposed to know fancy dinners and wine aren't the way to my heart?

Isn't that what tonight's supposed to be about? Getting to know one another. Figuring out what makes the other one tick.

Luca swings around the table and pulls out my chair, his eyes locked on me, much to the dismay of the hostess who has not stopped trying to impress him since we walked in.

But I mean, who could blame her?

Luca is gorgeous. Dressed in cashmere and designer jeans, he screams cocky pretty boy with money. But that's not what stands out to me. It's the stubble he didn't shave, because he knows I like it. It's the way he bites the inside of his cheek to hide his nerves, because he doesn't want to mess this up for any of us—Zach, me, or him. It's the way he looks at my son, like he is the center of his world. The way he looks at me—with the sort of intensity you expect from someone who is your ride or die.

But isn't that essentially what co-parenting is? Or at least it should be. For the rest of Zach's life, we're in this together.

I search his stubbled face, watching as his brow furrows.

"Is everything okay?" he asks, concern lacing his tone.

I nod, saving my spiraling thoughts for an in-depth evaluation later in the comfort of my own bed.

"Look at you being a gentleman," I quip in an attempt to lighten the mood. "Is this how you treat all the girls in LA?"

The joke hits its mark, and Luca chuckles as he rounds the table. "You assume I take them to dinner."

He tips the hostess and requests for a bottle of their finest red to be brought to the table. She, of course, asks if there's anything else she can do for him, but his eyes never stray from mine, encouraging me to keep questioning him.

So I do.

"You've got a new girl on your arm for every club opening and gala you attend. You're telling me there's not dinner involved?"

His shrug is paired with a smirk. "Sure, there's food when we attend those events. But there aren't dinners like this."

"And by that, you mean?"

He lowers his voice to an all too sexy octave. "Alone."

"I find that hard to believe," I counter with a disbelieving grin. The man is one of the most eligible bachelors on the west coast. There's no way he expects me to believe all those women are just arm candy, and he doesn't actually date them.

"Believe it. This"—he points between the two of us—"is not the norm. What we did in New York, that's the norm."

An awkward silence washes over the table as a bubbly blonde server returns with our wine. She introduces herself as Wendy and makes a show of leaning over to pour my glass, showing Luca her tits and gushing about how it's locally sourced at her father's vineyard down the mountain.

I have to fight back my laugh as Luca chews his cheek to stifle an irritated groan.

"Thanks," I tell Windy or Waverly. Whatever her name is. "We'll need a few minutes to look at the menu."

Ignoring me completely, she places a well-manicured hand on Luca's shoulder and coos, "Take all the time you need."

When she's gone, I glance in her direction. "Should I let her know there's an empty spot in your bed?"

"Why? Are you jealous?"

"Of her?" I ask. "Not at all."

"Good, because you shouldn't be," he reassures me, his gaze locked on mine as if he's determined to make sure I'm hearing him. He goes quiet, and then the corner of his mouth tips upward in a sexy half grin. "But if you were, what would you do?"

"I'd make sure she knows you're mine." It's a simple answer, one I haven't had to think about in years, considering that's how long it's been since I've been in any kind of serious relationship. But I'm the first to admit I'm territorial when it comes to what's mine.

"And just how would you do that?"

"Are you guys just about ready?" Winifred returns point two seconds after being dismissed, with her big brown eyes locked on Luca like she stands a chance.

I'm about to roll my eyes dramatically when I'm struck with a better plan.

"Actually, Wednesday, I think we're good."

She glares at me, a fake smile plastered on her Barbie pink lips. "It's Wendy."

"Right. We'll just take the check."

"We will?" Luca questions, an amused glint in his eye.

"Absolutely," I confirm, setting my menu down matter-of-factly. "After careful review, it's clear you're not going to find anything you like here."

"We are a five-star restaurant, ma'am. I'm sure there's *something* for him available."

"Maybe so, but it has nothing on the five-star pussy he's going to eat at home."

Luca's jaw drops like he isn't sure he heard me correctly. But when I meet his gaze, daring him to defy me, he doesn't hesitate. He stands and throws a hundred-dollar bill on the table. "Thanks, Winona."

The server stomps her foot and crosses her arms, heaving her tits skyward. "It's Wendy."

The guy at the table nearest us gives a slow clap as Luca wraps his hand around my bicep and hurls me from the chair. I struggle to keep up as he leads me out of the restaurant, but not before I look over my shoulder and wink at our still gaping server.

That'll teach her to mess with another woman's man.

Not that Luca's really mine, but seriously, what kind of girl's girl hits on a guy, who is out with another woman, right in front of her?

By the time we're out the door, I'm giggling like a schoolgirl. "Did you see her face?"

I glance up, only to find Luca isn't laughing.

He's not even smiling.

His hand loosens and brushes down my arm until he's wrapping his arm around my waist.

I gasp as he tugs me against him. Each point where we are connected feels magnetic—like lighting in a bottle fighting to get free. Goosebumps rise on my flesh and heat coils in my lower belly. It's simultaneously too much and everything I need at the same time.

"Luca…" My words are a plea for as I try to tug free of his grasp. Though I'm not sure exactly what I'm begging.

That only spurs him to tighten his grip, and splaying his fingers across my back, he presses his hips to mine.

Fuck, he's hard. Right here in the middle of the street, he's showing me just how turned on he is.

"Do you have any idea how incredibly fucking sexy that was?"

"What?" I breathe, double-checking to make sure I heard him correctly.

"I have never had a woman stake her claim like you just did."

"Never?"

"Not once."

I want to ask how that's possible. I want to believe him, but there's no way women haven't clawed their way to keep him in their beds.

"Women want me for what I can give them. They want press releases and fancy presents." His voice waivers under ragged breaths. "They don't stake their claim because they give a shit."

I call bullshit.

"And you think I do?" It's sarcasm at its finest, and we both know it.

Luca leans in until his lips are a hair's breadth from mine. "I know you do. You don't do anything by halves, but also, you're dressed in me. For you, that's practically yelling you want this."

My chest heaves against him. He's right. It wasn't enough for waitress Whitney to get the hint. I needed her to know he wasn't available. Just like I knew exactly what I was doing when I chose this jacket.

But I don't want this because of who he is outside of Telluride. Or because I know exactly how good his dick feels inside me.

I want this because he's gone above and beyond to show me he's changed. He's one of the good ones.

People pass on either side of us, giving a wide berth to the couple having a moment in the middle of the sidewalk, but we're living in the silence that hangs between us. I close my eyes, afraid that if I meet his gaze, I won't be able to stop myself from crossing the weakening line between us.

But he needs to know.

"You deserve someone to fight for you."

Luca tenses, and I immediately know, despite my good intentions, I've said the wrong thing.

Slamming my eyes open, I watch as Luca tears his gaze from mine and retreats into himself.

He steps back, and I instantly miss the feel of him against me. "We should get you fed."

"Luca—"

"Do you mean it?" The desperation in his voice kills me, even as it confirms there are pieces to this situation I'm missing. "Any of it. All of it. Do you mean it?"

I shoot him a light-hearted grin meant to reassure him. "Which part? That you have a delicious pussy to eat at home or that I'd fight for you?"

"Both."

I look him dead in the eye, just like he does when he wants to make sure I'm hearing him.

"Every word."

Chapter Nineteen

LUCA

The way I see it, we have two choices.

Pretend Leigh didn't just offer to let me devour her sweet cunt and instead eat a real meal here in town, or throw her over my shoulder and get her pretty little ass back on the gondola to a very empty guesthouse.

I know which I'd prefer.

Even if it is counterproductive to the reason I brought her out tonight.

The plan was to let her in. To tell her the truth. If I wasn't nervous as hell before, I am now. I'm fucking terrified to admit I'm not as put together as I pretend to be. And after Leigh all but claimed me in front of an entire restaurant, now she's looking up at me with those full red lips that I know look incredible wrapped around my cock. Why the hell would I choose to talk?

Leigh huffs an adorable laugh and takes a step forward. "Stop thinking so hard, Luca."

"I would if I could, but I'm not sure what to think." It's the understatement of the year.

She weaves her arms around my waist and, with all the confidence she's been missing, says, "Let's just take it one moment at a time. How about that?"

I don't react. Don't sweep her up in my arms like I'm dying to. "What does that mean? Because you're confusing the hell out of me. I'm not sure if this is a test and I'm supposed to walk away, or if you really want me."

Her tongue darts out and wets her bottom lip. "It's not a test."

"Fuck, Little Thief." I breathe, my breath forming a cloud between us. "I need you to tell me what you want."

Her glacier eyes flash with hunger as she lifts her hands and loops them around my neck. "I've done a lot of thinking today. A lot of reflecting. And right now, I want you to take me home, Luca."

Hope blooms in my chest. Followed by vivid images of all the things I've only let myself consider in dreams.

This is really happening.

I don't know what the hell all her thinking and reflecting has to do with it, because all I hear is she wants me.

Me.

I swallow past the rising emotion in my throat and give her one last chance to stop this. "What about our talk?"

The last thing I want to do is fuck this up. I need to know I'm not overstepping. Not pushing too hard, or too fast.

"Words are just words, and the past is the past. Eventually, I want your story, but you've shown me the man you are now and that's enough for me."

That's all the encouragement I need.

My hands tangle in her hair and my mouth slants over hers. She doesn't hesitate to open for me.

I groan as our tongues tangle, and Leigh grinds her hips against my already painfully hard cock.

"Oh, fuck," I growl and, lowering my hands to the round of her perfect ass, I lift her, wrapping her legs around my waist.

Leigh grinds against me as she peppers kisses along my jaw, each one a lightning strike lighting me up from the inside out. God, this woman is everything. When she reaches my ear, she sucks the lobe between her teeth and slowly tugs until I'm whimpering from the mix of pain and pleasure.

"We should probably get off the sidewalk," Leigh whispers. "Unless you want the fine people of Telluride to see me come."

"Shit. I've missed that filthy mouth of yours."

I might not know exactly how we got here, but she's right. I'm not about to let anyone else witness the things I'm going to do to her.

Thank God we're only around the corner from the gondola station.

Not bothering to set her down, I hightail it in that direction.

Leigh laughs and presses her lips to my neck, nibbling on the sensitive flesh. My hips jerk, dick flexing against the heat of her pussy, and she lets out a soft moan.

"You're going to pay for that, Little Thief."

"I'm looking forward to it," she purrs.

There's no line when we reach the station. Most people are heading into town instead of back to their cabins. The attendant shoots me an arched brow but doesn't comment on the fact I'm carrying Leigh as we cross the threshold into the mostly glass cube. There's a bench on each side and a handrail on the ceiling, and all I can think about is how amazing she'd look hanging from them while I pounded my cock into her sweet pussy.

There's no light in the gondola except for the faint light of the city behind us and the moon rising over the crest of the mountains. It's beautiful, but not as gorgeous as the woman in my arms.

I mentally calculate our route home. It's a long ride to the top. Fifteen minutes, to be exact.

That's more than enough time.

I set Leigh down and step forward, pushing until her thighs are backed against the bench with the mountainside behind her. Cupping her face with both hands, I force myself to memorize everything about her in this moment—every line, every freckle, every bit of heat in her icy blue eyes.

"You're beautiful," I whisper. "I don't think I told you that tonight."

Her eyes dart to my lips and back. "Thank you. So are you."

Fuck, I love it when she thanks me.

I trail my hands from her cheeks, down her collarbones, and over her tits inside my jacket, barely grazing my thumbs against her already taught nipples.

Her body comes to life under my touch, and she lets out a breathy moan. "What are you doing?"

Dipping lower, down past her hips, I finger the edge of her dress. "Do you want me to stop?"

"No. Don't," she begs, her body jolting with a shiver. "Please, don't stop."

"Oh, Little Thief, you have no idea what you're giving me." I drop to my knees and tip my head back, savoring her parted lips and the shock on her face. "Because I won't stop. Not until I've stolen all the orgasms I've missed."

My hands slip beneath her skirt, and Leigh moans as I knead her nylon clad thighs.

"Here? Right now?"

"Because this is any different than up against a vending machine?" I ask, fingers inching toward her core.

She moans, but doesn't stop me when I push up her skirt and find both her nylons and emerald green lace panties soaking wet. It seems my girl is still turned on by our little bouts of exhibitionism.

"Tell me to stop and I will."

"Anyone could look up and see." Her voice is soft and raw, but it's a weak protest only further disproven by the way she widens her legs to make room for me.

A devilish grin tips my lips. "Then I'll just have to make sure I'm quick."

I press my face into her pussy and breathe in deep, scenting her like a feral animal. And when it comes to her, maybe I am.

"Luca, please." Her voice trembles.

Fuck, I love it when she begs.

"Please what, Little Thief?"

I nip at her clothed cunt, taking her nylons between my teeth, and grind them with my canines. Not enough to tear—not yet. She might not need my words, but hers give me fucking life.

"Yes," she moans, lifting her hips to find friction but coming up empty. "Please, I want you to make me come."

I jerk my head, ripping the fabric with ease and moan at the sight. Her panties aren't just emerald green lace. They've got a little red bow at the top, with a mistletoe charm hanging right above her clit.

"Fuck me," I groan. "Did you wear these just for me?"

She giggles. "I might have picked them up at the Christmas market today in a moment of mania. But when I put them on this evening, it was definitely with you in mind."

"God damn, Leigh. You can't find your Christmas spirit and then say shit like that. I'm liable to bend you over right now and pound the daylights out of this sweet little cunt."

"Tsk, tsk," she clicks her tongue. "For someone who loves Christmas, I thought you'd know how mistletoes works."

I can't stop the growl that breaks free from my chest.

The little grinchy minx. She doesn't even know the weight of what she's done.

Leigh reaches down and runs her fingers through my hair. "Now be a good boy and kiss me under the mistletoe."

My cock jolts as I utter an emphatic, "Yes, ma'am."

Pulling the lacey fabric to the side, I part her smooth lips with two fingers and throw up a silent prayer of thanks to any and every god imaginable. Her pussy is gorgeous—pink and full, and mine.

Yup, I'm pretty sure this is what my heaven looks like.

Her knees tremble as I run my tongue from bottom to top, forcing her hand to dart from my head to the railing above her for balance.

The image is even sexier than I envisioned—hands grasping the bar like it's a lifeline, all the while keeping her lust filled gaze on me.

Holding her gaze, I suck her clit between my teeth and sink two fingers inside.

Her pussy clenches around me as she moans my name, followed by a few incoherent curses.

I hum against her skin. "Fuck, you're so damn tight."

"Imagine what it will feel like when it's your dick," Leigh whimpers.

This damn woman is trying to kill me.

And at this point, I'll go willingly.

Hard and fast, I flick a staccato rhythm with my tongue against her clit, matching my fingers thrust for thrust.

"Oh!" she mewls and lifting her leg, she practically climbs onto my shoulders, hips thrusting in search of more friction.

"Luca!" she cries, a hint of panic in her voice as the gondola swings from our movement. "I'm going to fall."

If she thinks I'm going to stop for anything short of a hurricane sending us falling to our death, she's dead wrong.

Her pussy clenches around my two fingers, and I know she's close. Flicking, sucking, and teasing her clit with my tongue, I slip my hand from inside her and wrap my arms around her thighs and lift her.

She understands my silent request and tangles her hands in my hair so I can slowly lower her to the bench behind her, my lips never parting from the woman who drives me wild.

As soon as she's safely seated, I replace my fingers inside her and I raise my other hand to pull the top of her dress down, freeing her perfect tits.

Looking up from between her legs, I groan as her chest heaves. I palm her breast, my thumb tracing circles over her rosy, peaked nipple.

They're utterly fucking perfect. And goddamn, do they look spectacular in my hands.

Leigh jerks her hips and whimpers, "Luca, I'm gonna—"

Before she can finish that statement, her whole body tenses, signaling she's right where I want her—on the edge, waiting for me to take her there. Committing this moment to memory, I pull her nipple away from her chest and add a third finger to her pussy.

That does it.

Leigh tightens her hold in my hair and grinds herself against my talented tongue. She rides my face through her orgasm, and it's easily the sexiest thing I've ever experienced. The way she lets me pleasure her, but has no qualms about taking what she needs in the moment. It takes everything in me not to give into my aching cock and come in my pants.

"Oh my God," she whispers, limbs shaking as she comes down from her pleasure and all but squirming to get away from my face.

"I'm not done," I growl against her, pinning her against the bench.

"But—"

"One more. Give me one more before we get to the top."

"I can't. It's too sensitive," she says, but her pretty little blue eyes, alight with lust, tell a different story. They like what I'm saying. They're begging for me to make good on my word.

"Then you'll come fast and hard," I taunt. "Come on. I want you to drown me, Little Thief."

I suck her clit and roll the sensitive bud between my teeth, desperate to make her orgasm at my hands and mouth one more time before we reach the top of this damn mountain.

"Oh," she cries, pulling at my hair. "Yes, Luca. Right there."

I curl my fingers, stroking the tips against the spot that drives her wild. I look up and watch her come undone. She's got her head thrown back, tits heaving in the moonlight. In short, she's fucking gorgeous, and I never want this moment to end.

My dick throbs painfully against my zipper. Angry he's not getting any attention, but he'll have his time. This moment is for Leigh—and creating a vivid memory that will live rent free in my mind until the day I die.

"Luca—fuck—your fingers—God, right there—I'm going to—"

God, I love that filthy mouth of hers.

Her pussy pulses around my fingers, her second orgasm taking hold of her shuddering body. It starts in her toes as she flexes them and straightens her legs tight against my cheeks. When it reaches her core, she curls forward, holding on as long as she can without giving in.

Well, that just won't do.

I pinch her nipple, rolling it tight between my fingers.

"Oh, Luca," she yells. "Yes!"

My name on her lips drives me wild, and I growl against her clit, working my mouth and fingers until her only option is to shatter for me.

And she does.

So. Fucking. Beautifully.

Every muscle she has pulses and releases at the same time, flooding my mouth with the delicious taste of her. She cries my name, over and over, the waves of pleasure crashing through her.

She goes limp against the seat, and I take my time cleaning up every inch of what's mine. When I finally look up, I'm greeted with a lazy, almost drunk smile painted on her face.

"That was…incredible."

"You absolutely were."

"Please tell me we're not done."

"Not even close, Little Thief." I stand up, licking my lips so I can taste every last drop of her. "Now let's get you covered up. We're almost to the top and as much as almost getting caught turns me on, I have zero desire to let anyone else see what's mine."

It's a bold statement.

But when she doesn't correct me, my heart begins to beat for her alone.

Chapter Twenty

LEIGH

I wake up in the darkened bedroom in the guesthouse, unsure of three things:

How I got from the gondola to here.

When I passed out.

How long I've been asleep.

What I do know:

My thighs are raw from the scruff of Luca's jaw.

When I think about what happened, my pussy twitches with the need for a repeat performance.

God, that was the best orgasm I've ever had.

Scratch that. The best two orgasms.

If I had known last time that Luca could do all that with his tongue, I would have demanded he get on his knees instead of the other way around.

I curl into the fluffy duvet and take stock of the pure satisfaction radiating from my body. I'd almost forgotten what it felt like to come at the hands of a man. Let this serve as a reminder never to let the cobwebs take over again. Luca knows what the hell he's doing.

Speaking of Luca…

I roll over, finding no trace of my maybe baby daddy.

God, that's still such a weird thing to admit—even in the silence of my own mind. But surprisingly, I don't hate it.

My eyes drift to the clock on the nightstand, and I almost choke. It's nearly ten o'clock. I've slept for two hours.

Does that mean Zach is in his room? Or is he still in the main house? Shit.

Scrambling to get up, I all but fall out of the bed only to realize I'm in nothing but an oversized Monarchs shirt that may or may not be Luca's. No panties in sight.

And he calls me a thief.

I eye a set of sleep shorts draped over the chair in the corner, and then, in a manic attempt at being sexy, forgo them all together. Hopefully Luca didn't invite the guys to come over, otherwise this could get real awkward, real fast.

Zach's room is void of any sign of him. It's not until I'm almost to the living room that I'm hit with a delicious smell and the sound of someone softly singing *Santa Baby*.

He's off key and makes up the words he can't remember, but it's the spirit of it that melts my heart. This man has so many sides to him. Many of them he doesn't let people see. I understand why he doesn't do more than dinners with women or invite them to this sacred holiday. If they saw even a fraction of what I have this week, they'd never let him go.

When I round the corner into the main room, Luca is standing at the kitchen island. Still in his jeans and cashmere sweater, he plates what looks like some kind of pasta.

"Is there any of that left over for me?"

He looks up, and I'm struck by the little smirk on his lips and the way his blue eyes shine with a hint of mischief.

"This is for you. I wasn't sure when you were going to wake up, but I wanted to make sure you had food when you did."

"Oh." My shock slips free. I can't remember the last time I had a man cook for me. Like really cook for me. Not like Bash offering me breakfast he was already going to make anyway, but having the foresight to make sure I'm fed.

It's a nice feeling.

I cross over the tiny living room to the kitchen and slide onto the barstool. "What is it?"

Luca slides the plate in front of me and turns to grab a fork. "Chicken tequila fettuccine with roasted peppers."

"And you made this?"

"Don't act so surprised. I might have grown up as a pretentious douche, but I really like to eat. So once I was on my own, I forced myself to learn a few dishes. Just don't ask me to cook breakfast. I'll burn the eggs every time."

"I think I can handle breakfast."

"Are you offering?"

"Maybe if you're lucky." I wink.

Luca makes a plate for himself and slides onto the stool next to mine. "And what does a guy have to do to get lucky?"

I pick up my fork and twirl the noodles around it. "First, you can tell me where my son is."

"He's in the house. Enzo has the monitor and offered to give you the night off."

"He might be in the running for favorite twin."

Luca lifts a brow in surprise, his posture straightening. "Not the twin whose name you were screaming mere hours ago?"

I pause, my fork halfway to my mouth, as I shrug playfully. "I'll admit he's unforgettable."

"I'll take it…for now."

His words silently suggest I'm going to pay for my comment, and excitement courses through me.

I finally take a bite and the moment it touches my tongue, I let out a long, low moan.

Tangy yet savory, it's quite possibly the best pasta I've ever tasted.

He sucks in an audible breath. "Keep doing that and I'll forget that you need to eat before I wreck that little body of yours."

My eyes go wide, and I can't help but clench my thighs.

Luca tracks the movement and groans. "For fuck's sake. Eat, Leigh."

A laugh bubbles out of me, and I relish in the ease we've found with one another.

As we continue to eat, the conversation flows like the wine he pours us. He tells me about the Monarchs' team line up for next season, and I tell him about my plans for Renegade Hearts. He laughs when I tell him about the smutty book club I have with Willow and Indie, claiming that's where my dirty mouth must have come from, and I cackle when he tells me about the time Holt and Bash convinced him to run naked through the streets of Monaco during a rainstorm.

By the time we're both done, my cheeks hurt from smiling so much. It's been so long since I've gotten the chance to just be me. Not Zach's mom. Not Willow's partner. Just Leigh. And Luca makes it effortless. His wit and sarcasm are on par with my own, and he doesn't fault me for finding the logic in every situation. But most of all, he calls me on my bullshit the same way I do him.

I never imagined it could be this way between us.

It's both exciting and terrifying.

It's late when Luca reaches over and intertwines his fingers with mine, sending my heart into a thunderous fit in my chest.

"I really want to kiss you again," he admits, his gaze falling to my lips.

I counter with a flirtatious smile. "I really want to do more than kiss you."

"Fuck," he groans, covering his eyes with his free hand. "I want that too."

It sounds like there's a follow-up. A "but" that is going to ruin this peaceful moment.

"But before I can do all the things I want with you tonight"—he lifts my hand and presses a kiss to my knuckles—"I need to tell you everything."

His eyes meet mine, and I'm not surprised to see the vulnerability in his blue depths. Luca is nothing if not thorough. He and his best friends might be complete frat boys, but they are honest in a way that is undeniably noble. You want to hate them for it, but you can't.

"Okay." I nod, leaning back on the barstool.

He needs this.

We need this.

I slide our hands to my lap, cupping my free hand over them. "Tell me your story."

Luca inhales a steadying breath, and I give a reassuring squeeze before he starts.

"Family has always been the most important thing to me. Probably because mine was such a damn farce."

"The Donatis? A farce?" I feign disbelief, lifting my free hand to clutch my imaginary pearls. "I don't believe it."

"I know. Who would have thought? But it's true, the golden family of Shady Grove is anything but. Especially back when your family came to town."

I still in confusion. "Mine?"

His mouth twitches, and I'd bet money he's biting his cheek. "Your dad challenged the way things were done in town. He might not have been in the hotel business like the Donatis, but he was new money coming into a well-oiled machine he knew nothing about. Everyone loved him, and therefore everyone loved you and your mom too."

"You didn't," I sneer, remembering the way he used to scrunch up his nose in disgust.

"Oh, that's where you're wrong, Little Thief."

"I hate that you call me that still."

"You do?"

"Yes, and no." I pause, trying to find the right explanation. "While it's incredibly sexy when we've lost our minds and our clothes, it reminds me of what you did, and I'm not sure that's what I want to remember now."

He huffs a laugh, but I don't follow what's so funny. "Do you want to know why I call you that?"

"Isn't it obvious? Because *you* framed me for stealing your mother's locket."

"I did." He nods, wearing a cheshire grin. "But that's not why I call you that."

My eyes flash with confusion. "Then why?"

"Because while you may not have stolen the locket, you stole a part of me when you came to town."

"What?" My voice is a broken whisper.

"Do you remember the first time we met?"

I shake my head. "No."

"You came over for my sister's fifteenth birthday. It was the first week of summer, and I was annoyed I had to stick around to celebrate with ten boy crazed teenage girls. I was in the kitchen after a morning run, and you ran straight into me trying to find some of—what did you call it—the magical bean water?"

My mouth drops open as I recall the moment. He was gorgeous even back then. All the girls at that party wanted him and Enzo. I was just happy to be included. Going away to boarding school with Willow and Indie, I didn't know many of the girls in Shady Grove. Luca's sister was my first and only friend in town.

"I can't believe you remember that?"

His smile grows impossibly wider. "Down to the pink panda pajamas you were wearing."

"You must have been what—nineteen?"

He nods. "It was the last summer Enzo and I spent at home."

"Why?"

"I'll get to that," he promises, running his thumb along my forefinger. "That morning, you bestowed upon me the gift of what I found out later was referred to as Leigh's Story Time. Apparently, you wouldn't shut up about your family or how amazing they were."

My stomach sinks. "They were."

"You don't talk about them much anymore."

"It hurts to." As much as I want to pretend it doesn't, it does. I've made peace with their deaths, but I don't think it will ever hurt not to think about them and all the things I'll never get to do with them.

"I'm sorry." He gives my hand a squeeze, and I glance up. "That morning you told me about how you started drinking coffee just so you could share twenty minutes alone with your mom in the morning before your dad would wake up. You loved talking about the day ahead with her."

Tears prick the corners of my eyes, and my gaze falls to the bracelet Luca bought me at the Christmas market.

"You knew when you bought this?"

I loved those mornings with my mom. There isn't a morning that goes by that I don't wish she was there with me, doing her crossword puzzles, ready to hand out sound advice or just listen to me talk.

He nods solemnly, not a hint of playfulness in his expression.

"I—I don't know what to say. How does any of this add up to stealing a part of you?"

"Because I was jealous," Luca rasps, pulling his hand from mine. He runs it through his silky black hair and sighs. "So fucking jealous."

"Of me?"

He nods again and I swear there are tears in his eyes too. "You have to understand, my parents didn't believe in anything but preserving the Donati name. That was their full-time job. We didn't get moments like that. We got nannies and tutors, impersonal birthday gifts and, if we were lucky, a hug on Christmas. I always had a little more than that because I had a twin to hold on to, but that morning you showed me what a family could be. And I wanted it."

Luca looks away, shaking his head over and over, and my heart breaks for him.

I reach for his hand, but he snatches it back.

"The rest of that summer, I listened to my mother and father complain about your dad getting involved in Shady Grove, but mostly I watched you. I listened to you tell my sister stories of your adventures with your mom and dad. I watched you at all the fundraisers, carefree and twirling in your beautiful summer dresses, dancing with your father. I became obsessed, but also so fucking angry that I'd never know what it was like to be loved by a parent like that."

"God, Luca, I'm sorry," I whisper.

Luca huffs a laugh. "Why are you apologizing? You did absolutely nothing wrong."

"No, I didn't, but that doesn't mean I can't hate the shitty behavior of your parents."

"Oh, it gets worse." He spits out like venom, but it's not directed at me.

"Go on."

"My parents decided something needed to be done to take your family down a peg, and they knew they couldn't touch your father. Shady Grove loved him too much."

"So you went after me," I conclude, my voice nothing more than a shattered whimper.

"Fuck, Leigh." Luca takes my hands, desperation radiating from his strong grip. "Please look at me."

I drag my gaze to meet his, praying he doesn't see the hatred in my eyes and mistake it for being directed at him. Because while he may have been the one who pulled the trigger, he didn't aim the gun. His parents did.

Luca brings our hands to his lips and presses a kiss to my palm. "I'm not proud of what I did. I just—I thought if I did something to help, my parents would finally see me. Maybe they would invite me to the adult table and trust me with family affairs. I just wanted to be more than the son they could advantageously marry off."

"Were they proud of you?" I ask, needing a silver lining to make it all worth it. "After you framed me."

"For a time." He pauses. "Then Enzo and I were drafted."

"For the majors?"

He nods. "Our parents didn't even know we'd been scouted. They never showed up to a single game. Baseball wasn't one of their approved activities since it didn't benefit us when it came to following in their footsteps and taking a role in the family business."

"But you didn't do any of that."

"No. When Enzo declared he had no desire to play Major League ball, I opted out, too, and convinced everyone I wanted to play college ball, so I'd have a degree to fall back on. The two of us went on to play at Stonewall, much to our parent's dismay."

"Which is where you met Holt, Bash, and Jack."

"Exactly." He exhales a dry laugh. "And I'm grateful every day we did."

"I feel like I'm still missing a piece of the puzzle. Yesterday you said you didn't go home for Christmas that year, and I vaguely remember there being a stir up around that time over you and Enzo, but I was already the black sheep in town, so our family didn't hear much."

Luca frowns, and there's nothing soft about the way he grits out, "That would be right about when our family disowned us."

"What!" I jerk back, my anger rising for him. "How the hell did we miss that?"

He waves his hand mockingly with a fairy godmother flair. "Because, to my mother, appearances are everything."

God, what it must have been like to grow up in a house like that. Where everything you did was viewed under a microscope, but ultimately it didn't matter because it wasn't good enough. Then to be disowned. I can't even imagine.

"What happened?" I ask, because now I need to know how and why he broke free.

"When we declined the draft, my parents assumed it was because we would be taking over the family business. Enzo had zero desire to run hotels or become a politician and make backdoor deals with every lobbyist from Michigan to DC."

"And you?"

"Needed to make sure Enzo was set, but still had every intention of entering the draft after college."

"Let me guess, your parents were not happy about that."

"Smart girl," he says, tipping his head at me. "My parents proceeded to pull out every stop—from bribes to blackmail—but my stubborn ass twin wouldn't budge. It even got to the point where they agreed to allow me to play baseball if I could get my brother to come back to Shady Grove and keep with their perfect little plan."

"A stupid plan, really. Even I know you would never betray your brother like that."

"Exactly." He nods in agreement. "And at that point, we already had Jack and the guys, and we were beginning to see what a family you choose could look like."

"But you still want your family."

He ignores my question, but I don't need an answer. I can see it plain on his face when he talks about them. He's been hurt and betrayed by them, but this man has all the loyalty of a golden retriever. If Enzo said he wanted to go back to Shady Grove, Luca would be the bridge. He can't help it.

"Leigh." He waits until my eyes meet his and continues. "I am so sorry for what I did to you and all the pain I caused. I was stupid and reckless, and you didn't deserve any of it. I know you don't trust me. I wouldn't trust me either, but fuck, I hope someday you can learn to. Because I meant it when I said family is the most important thing to me. And like it or not, you might be a part of that now. I want you to be a part of it."

Luca offers me a smile, but again his eyes betray him.

He wants it all. His brother and what they've built together. The family that disowned him. And me. He's been chasing this dream since he was nineteen.

It's a dream I know all too well.

Because I've been chasing the same thing since my parents died. Latching on to Indie and Willow. Throwing myself into all the events and camps for Renegade Hearts. And, holding on as tightly as I can to Zach.

The question is, do I want to be a part of this? If Zach is his, or even if he isn't, do I want to explore this?

It's a simple answer with complicated roots.

Maybe it's the wine. Or maybe it's my exhausted heart. But I find myself nodding my head.

"Is that a yes?" There's hope in his voice, and I can't be the one to douse it.

Not right now.

Maybe not ever.

Because I do want *this*. I'm just not sure what *this* looks like long term.

I reach up and cup his face, running my fingertips down his stubbled jaw. "I don't know what guarantees I can make, but I can give you my forgiveness, and I can promise you one day at a time."

"Is that a yes?"

God, how is this man so complicated and so pure at the same time?

I laugh to myself. "Yes, I want this."

"Oh, thank God," he sighs and leans in, pressing his lips to mine. "It would have been so awkward to have to head back into the house and jack off in the shower alone."

"Oh, to be a fly on the wall."

I press my lips together as his smile grows. "You want to see me jack off?"

Picking up my glass of wine, I swirl it around, feigning amusement. "I don't know why men are so surprised by that? You'd love to watch me finger myself."

He barks a laugh. "Without a doubt."

"So why is it a shock that I'd want to watch you stroke, what I happen to know is, a cock meant to ruin women?"

"So tell me, Little Thief." The nickname sends a shiver down my spine. Knowing the meaning, knowing that he sees me not as a thief of trinkets but rather his heart, has me clamoring to hear it over and over. "What is it you want from me?"

"You like asking me that question."

"I do," he tells me, hand gripping my thigh under my sleep shorts. "I like when you tell me what to do. I like pleasing you. I also like spanking your ass when you piss me off."

Images from our night pressed up against the vending machine flash through my mind, and if his smile is any indication, he's thinking of it too.

This is a new concept for me. And as much as I love reading about men dominating their women, there is something so inherently sexy about the way my directions bring Luca to his knees. I don't hate it. In fact, I think it might be a part of me that's always been there I've just never explored. Mostly, I just have no idea what I'm doing.

"Don't think about it too hard." He slides his hand up and traces the outline of my pussy. "Tell me what you want. I'll give it to you. Then I'll take what I need. Balance."

Balance.

The best of both worlds.

I think I can get behind that.

Straightening my spine, I take a deep breath.

"Strip for me." I hear myself speak with more confidence than I've ever had in the bedroom. My voice is a low rasp and undeniably sexy. "Then I want you to stroke what is mine, until you're so close it hurts. But don't you dare come. That belongs only to me."

Luca's breath hitches, and he digs his nails into my thigh.

It's sharp and quick, eliciting a low hiss from me.

And then he's gone, stepping back to follow my orders.

With every move, he keeps his lust-filled eyes locked on mine, and my pussy clenches with need.

God, who am I?

And why am I so fucking turned on?

Chapter Twenty One

LUCA

I am so fucking hard for this woman.

She's everything.

Fuck, if she'd let me put a ring on her finger right now, I would.

I still can't believe this is real.

After everything I just shared, she still wants me.

It's like I'm living in a twilight zone of weird fantasies I never expected to have—but really, it's just the day before Christmas Eve, and Leigh is asking me to jack off for her.

Merry fucking Christmas to me.

Towering over her, I lean in and press a kiss to her forehead before rounding the small accent sofa chair and stepping up onto the coffee table.

Can't strip without a stage, right?

Leigh chuckles and swivels the barstool to face me as I kick off my socks and shoes and do an elaborate spin for her.

I shoot her a wink. "Like what you see?"

"Eh." She shrugs nonchalantly. "I'd rather have less talking, and more fabric hitting the floor."

My jaw drops and my cock throbs. She's a fucking natural at this. If there was any question in my mind that Leigh might have a little dominance in her blood, she just squashed it.

While I wouldn't say I'm submissive, for her, I could be. That's not to say I'm not going to push back. I love pushing her buttons. And spanking her ass. But this, with her? It's refreshing and unbelievably sexy.

I give another spin and pull off my cashmere sweater, eager to give her everything she wants.

When I reveal the button-down underneath, Leigh lets out a soft groan.

"Lose the button-down too," she snaps, like this second layer of fabric is wrecking her every plan.

My brow raises. "Patience is a virtue."

"But it isn't one of mine," Leigh coos. "Lose it."

"Yes, ma'am."

Her pupils dilate at the honorific. Interesting. I make a mental note to come back to that later.

Moving my fingers to my shirt, I slide each button through its hole with painfully slow precision, watching as she hangs on my every move.

She sucks her lower lip between her teeth and narrows her gaze, waiting for me to slide the fabric from my shoulders.

Only I don't.

I let it hang, giving her just a sliver of skin down my chest and abdomen.

She wants me naked and exposed for her. I want her desperate and aching for me.

"Oh, you're a little tease, aren't you, baby?" she tsks.

I stumble mid spin and look over my shoulder, making sure I heard her correctly. I've never been one to like pet names for myself, but from her, that term of endearment has never sounded so damn good.

"I don't have to be." I suck my thumb into my mouth and proceed to draw a line down the center of my chest, stopping to finger each of the silver bars in my nipples before dragging it through the tuft of hair below my belly button. "Come play with me."

She shakes her head, but her eyes never stray from where I've hooked my thumb in my waistband. "Not until you're naked and begging me to come."

Say less.

I lower my hand to my belt, sliding it open and easing down the zipper of my pants. That is, until movement halts my action, and I glance up to watch as Leigh uncrosses her legs and props one up on the back of the accent chair in front of her. The move forces the shirt she's wearing—my shirt—to bunch around her hips, giving me a view of her perfect cunt.

My hand drops to trace the lump in my pocket that is the panties I stole from her earlier.

This is what karma looks like.

I did this to myself by keeping a reminder of our time in the gondola, and then again—just now—by teasing her.

And. I. Fucking. Love. It.

In one fluid movement, I push my jeans down and step out of them, all the while watching as she trails her fingertips up and down her thigh, dipping dangerously close to her drenched pussy each time.

Her gaze falls to my boxer briefs, and she licks her lips. "Take your dick out, Luca."

"Yes, ma'am." I obey, dragging them down until my cock springs free.

Leigh lets out a string of curses that register as nothing but praise. Her gaze takes me in and I'm living for it. I don't even need to touch myself. I just need her.

Her commands.

Her attention.

Her love.

Fuck.

If I could only be so lucky.

One day at a time.

That's what she said.

Don't get ahead of myself.

"Now show me how you fuck yourself." Her command grounds me, pulling me back from the edge of my almost spiral.

I suck in an audible breath as I wrap my hand around my swollen cock, wishing it was the soft, dainty fingers she's using to circle her clit.

"Look at you," she mumbles, almost to herself, desperate need shining in her eyes. "You're dripping."

"That's what you do to me," I reply through clenched teeth, running my fingers over the weeping head of my cock. "You reduce me to nothing more than a cum spigot."

"Fuck, Luca," she purrs. "That shouldn't be as hot as it is."

No, it shouldn't. But I'm learning anything and everything with Leigh turns me on.

Each stroke takes me closer to the edge until my balls tighten with the need to come.

Not yet.

I will not fail her.

I should have known I wouldn't last long. Between the gondola and this, I'm surprised I've lasted more than a few minutes.

Slowing down my pace, I force myself to breathe through the pleasure and not give in.

Leigh sits back, her fingers teasing her clit, as I work myself to the edge two more times.

"Tell me what you're thinking of as you jerk my cock," she commands, her voice somewhere between a whisper and a moan.

"Fuck." My hips jerk forward at her possessiveness, and I pant between jagged breaths. "You. I'm thinking of you."

Her brows shoot to her hairline and her fingers stop their

movement. "Me?"

I huff a strangled laugh. "As if it would be anyone else. You, sitting there with those pretty little fingers teasing yourself. You, clamping your thighs around my head in the gondola as you came on my tongue. You, pressed up against that vending machine screaming my name as I came deep within your cunt. Fuck Leigh, since then it's always been you."

Her eyes soften and when she smiles, and it almost ruins me.

I want all those smiles.

The kind that reaches her eyes.

It's at that moment I realize I might have ruined her life, but she's destroyed mine. There's no coming back from this moment. A life without Leigh will be like living in a black and white movie—satisfying but dull. Especially after having experienced technicolor.

"You're devastating when you're on the edge."

"What?" I was so lost in my thoughts I didn't track Leigh moving from the barstool

Now she's in front of me, close enough I can touch her, and lost in the sight of me stroking my cock.

Given her height, and the fact I'm standing on the coffee table, the warmth of her breath teases my dick as she speaks.

Desperation mounts in my chest. "Is that a good thing?"

"It's a magnificent thing. You're doing so fucking good."

My chest puffs out, preening under her praise.

She takes a step forward and drags her hand across my thigh to my ass, digging her nails into the supple flesh. "Are you aching for me, baby?"

"Yes," I whine. It takes everything in me not to reach for her. She hasn't said I can't touch her, but it feels like an unspoken rule. One I'm not going to break.

"Me too."

"What do you want?" My lust-filled voice shakes with need.

She traces her fingers back to the front of my thighs, moving painfully close to my dripping cock, but never touching it. "Oh, I want a great many things from you, Luca, but first, I want to taste you again."

"Oh, thank God," I blurt out, which earns me one of Leigh's adorable chuckles.

A smile stretches across her face as she pulls her hair back, and I immediately grab it to keep it out of the way as she prepares to choke on my dick.

Never let it be said I'm not a gentleman.

"You ready?" she asks, eyes full of anything but innocence.

"Yes, but fair warning I'm not going to—" My words die on my tongue when, in one single motion, Leigh licks my shaft from root to tip.

"Oh fuck," I exhale, not getting more than a moment before she's sliding my length into her warm, waiting mouth.

I groan, fisting her hair tighter as she bobs on my cock like it's a popsicle. She hollows her cheeks as she hits the back of her throat, and I know I'm not going to last.

"God, Leigh, just like that."

My hips thrust forward as I cradle her skull. "Best. Head. Ever," I grunt, punctuating each word with a thrust.

At that, she gives a hum of satisfaction around my shaft, sending vibrations straight to the depths of my balls.

I let out a strangled moan. "If you don't stop that right now, I'm going to come," I warn, but Leigh doesn't show any signs of slowing down.

She sucks and twirls her talented tongue until my thick and swollen shaft throbs in her mouth. Gripping my hips tight, she encourages me to pound her throat through my release.

Tingles shoot up my spine and I try to hold off, but it's no use. I fall off the edge, knowing damn well she's going to be there to catch me when I land.

Her eyes roll back as she milks every last drop from me.

It takes a moment for me to stop seeing stars. That was—there are no words.

Leigh beams and kisses a path down my shaft, sending a shiver of aftershocks through me.

"That was—" I breathe.

"The best head ever?" She chuckles, smug and satisfied.

"Without a doubt."

"Considering you put me into a coma with that tongue of yours, I had a standard to live up to."

My cock twitches at her high praise.

God, what this woman does to me.

I hop down from the coffee table, wobbling on my legs like a baby deer. Threading my arm around her waist, I lean in so my lips hover over hers. "And to think, I still have so many tricks up my sleeve you don't even know about."

She presses a soft kiss to my lips before pulling back, brow raised. "Is that right?"

"Oh, my Little Thief, since you've found your Christmas spirit tonight, I'm going to give you a Christmas miracle."

She swallows hard, but not before her tongue darts out to lick the tiny bit of cum at the corner of her lips. "You are?"

Her question is soft, almost adoring, like the tables have turned and she's waiting for me to take charge.

And I have never been more ready.

I look down at Leigh, her eyes wide in anticipation.

I reach out and tuck a stray blonde curl behind her ear, though it does nothing to tame the just-been-face-fucked state of her hair. "Absolutely. I'm going to ruin that sweet little pussy of yours. I'm going to fuck you so thoroughly that every time you think of sex, you'll think of Christmas.

You'll think of me."

A flash of fear crosses her face before she juts her chin out and, with all the confidence in the world, declares, "Maybe Christmas isn't so bad after all."

Damn straight.

"Now be a good girl and meet me in the bedroom. I want you naked, hands on the bed frame, and your ass on display for me."

Leigh lifts a hand and gives me a mock salute. "Yes, sir."

Yup.

It's official.

I love this woman.

Chapter Twenty-Two

LEIGH

The anticipation is killing me.

Or maybe it's that I still haven't come down from the high of watching Luca stroke himself for me.

Then there was the taste of him.

The feel of him—hard and throbbing. Someone please remind me never to go three years without dick again.

Or maybe it's Luca's dick.

Or just Luca.

I can't count the number of times I've said it this week, but he's nothing like I remember or imagined. The way he lets me take charge—lets me suck him dry after making him tease himself until he aches—then takes over and orders me to wait for him. The whiplash should be jarring, but it's not. It's everything I didn't know I needed.

All this time, I thought I needed to be told what I wanted. And don't get me wrong, sometimes I do. There are days I'm so exhausted from making decisions that it's nice to have someone tell me to sit down, spread my legs, and let them feast on my pussy.

Like right now.

My head spins with a million-and-one thoughts after that little display in the living room. Of course, my core is still dripping with the desire to be fucked, but I am so happy Luca decided to take over.

Give and take, that's what Luca said.

Balance.

The click of the door behind me alerts me to his presence.

I glance over my shoulder and wiggle my ass, unashamed that I'm fully naked and vulnerable for this man.

"Look at you," he purrs, his voice dripping with lust. "Waiting for me, kneeling like a good fucking girl. You're so goddamn beautiful, Leigh." As if to prove his point, he fists his already thickening cock, stroking it back to hard.

"You are too," I reply, my voice an anxious whisper.

The thing is a monster. My throat still carries the delicious ache of its presence, and if I didn't already know it would fit between my legs, I might be worried.

But that's not what has my heart hammering in my chest and butterflies taking flight in my abdomen.

It's the fact that everything about this feels different.

This is more than just a night in a vending machine closet. Tonight, we've shared more than just sex and orgasms. The hate between us is gone, and in its place is something fragile and new.

Luca declared his desire to claim me.

And the crazy part is—I want him to.

With his free hand, he brings a red foil packet to his lips and tears it open with his teeth.

I love that he didn't think twice. There wasn't a conversation on if we needed protection. It's like he knew there's no way in hell he'd be touching me without making sure all our bases were covered.

Pinching the tip, he rolls it down over his shaft and looks back up at me, his eyes dark and menacing.

"Touch yourself," he rasps. "Get yourself ready for me."

I don't dare tell him I'm already dripping.

The tiniest whimper escapes my lips as I part my legs further and press a finger to my clit. Sparks fly beneath my skin as I circle the sensitive bud, heat coiling deep in my core.

Luca slides onto the bed behind me and runs his hand over the round of my ass. "I've been dreaming about his ass since spring training."

I arch my back, leaning into his touch, and moan, "Yes."

He slides his fingers down, ghosting the edge of my throbbing cunt like the tease he is.

"You've made me wait so fucking long to touch you," Luca growls.

Craning my neck to see his face, I whimper, "Are you going to punish me?"

"Is that what you want?"

Luca digs his fingers into my hips, pulls me flush against his own. He slides his length through my slit and teases my clit. "Do you want me to take you over my knee and turn your ass the same color as Santa's suit?"

A desperate whimper escapes me as I rasp, "If you think it will help me remember that Christmas is sex and sex is you."

"Fucking hell. You already have my heart. Are you trying to steal more from me with that mouth of yours, my Little Thief?"

My. Little. Thief.

So possessive. So sexy. And to think I hated that nickname twenty-four hours ago.

"Don't worry, I'll keep all your things safe."

He exhales a groan as he splays his hand wide across my ass cheek.

"If at any point you want me to stop, all you have to do is say so."

"I won't."

"Leigh," he growls, "I need you to tell me you understand."

"I understand," I repeat, meeting his gaze with an underlying defiance.

He shakes with contained laughter, stifling what I'm sure would be an all too sexy grin.

I turn back to the headboard, gripping it tight, and wiggle my ass one more time for him. "Now please, baby. Punish me for keeping this tight little cunt from you. Break me. Ruin Christmas for me in the best possible way. Then put me back together so this moment will live rent free in my mind for years to come."

The next sound I hear is the crack of his hand against my ass. Pain and pleasure burst through me, and I let out a strangled gasp.

I whip my head around to find that grin plastered across Luca's face.

I was right. It's devastatingly sexy.

"That one's an extra for your cheeky commentary." He rubs his hand over the heated imprint he left behind. "Now count for me. I think five should be a good reminder."

"Yes, sir," I reply, playfully.

Luca shakes his head as he slips his hand between my legs and rubs his fingers through my pussy until they're soaked with my arousal.

My playful tone is replaced with a soft mewl.

SMACK!

He cracks his hand over the opposite cheek, evenly distributing his punishment.

"One," I cry out.

SMACK!

"Two."

He rubs my ass, soothing the tender flesh with his hand before once again teasing my aching cunt. Only this time, when he reaches the top, he uses two fingers to trace slow, deliberate circles over my clit.

I thrust my hips forward, searching for friction. The moment I find it, he withdraws his hand and delivers two swift slaps to my ass.

"Three, four," I manage through gritted teeth, frustrated that I was so close to coming and he tore it away from me.

Luca leans over, his panted breaths and stubble tickling my ear. "That orgasm is meant for my cock. I suggest you keep it safe for me."

Fuck, I cry internally. Both at the way he throws my words in my face and because I'm wound so fucking tight with the need to come, and he basically just challenged me not to.

And my parents didn't raise a quitter.

Craning my neck, I meet Luca's gaze and press a soft kiss to his lips. "Do your worst, Donati."

He sucks my lip between his teeth in response and pulls back slowly until my swollen flesh pops free, revealing a devilish smirk. "With pleasure."

That's when he gives it to me—the final smack.

I cry out the corresponding number, but it's cut short by Luca slamming his cock inside me to the hilt.

"Oh," I mewl, my release crashing over me like a wave meeting the shore.

"Fuck, Leigh, you're so damn tight." His voice cracks as he stills, giving me a moment to adjust to his size. "You should see yourself stretched around me. Like you were meant for me."

I take a deep breath, and Luca digs his fingers into my flesh like a man desperate to hold on. Shifting his hips, he slowly thrusts—each one longer and faster than the one before it.

"Oh God" slips from my lips.

"No. I'm Luca." He runs his hands from the heated flesh of my ass up the curves of my hips to my tits, squeezing them between his calloused fingers. "But make no mistake, I'm going to make you cry my name like a prayer and worship every inch of this gorgeous body."

He seals his promise with another thrust.

"Are you okay?"

I nod, unable to form a coherent sentence. The initial thrust was a shock, but now that he's inside me there's nothing but the delicious pinch of being filled.

"Good." He pistons his hips, pulling out to the tip and thrusting to the hilt.

Over and over, he lays claim to my body at a punishing pace, and I moan his name as he promised—like a litany of prayers.

I've never been fucked like this.

He's giving me everything he has. I'm at his mercy. And yet, I've never felt more cherished. Like my body is the only thing keeping him tethered to this reality.

It's mind-blowing.

I'm so close.

Right there.

And then he slows.

Luca's once hurried strokes become less frantic and more languid. Every inch of him is destroying me, but it's slow. Sensual. Searching.

His hands travel the length of my arms, intertwining his fingers in mine as he trails kisses along my spine to the shell of my ear.

"You are—I've wanted this for so long, Leigh."

I love when he calls me his Little Thief, but my name on his lips is raw.

It's real.

It's my undoing.

"Don't let me go," I whisper, and I realize I'm lost enough in this man that my subconscious is voicing my greatest fear.

Panic grips my spine, and I still in his arms, fighting to keep myself from running.

I've spent my entire adult life only letting in the people I know aren't going to leave me like my parents did. I know it's not the same. Death can happen at any moment, but I've protected my heart in every way possible from feeling that kind of loss again.

Luca has the power to break me like that. He has the freedom to walk away and take a piece of me with him.

As if reading my silent thoughts, he tightens his grip, so much so that I can feel his thundering heartbeat in time with mine. "I need you to hear me when I say this, Leigh. That's never going to happen."

I hear his words. I only wish I believed them.

Maybe with time.

Maybe if he stays.

I want him to stay.

Softly, Luca rocks us back, widening my legs so I'm straddling his lap. Every inch of us connected.

"Ride me, Leigh," he whispers. "Then come with me."

It's intimate.

It's terrifying.

It's perfect.

Giving me back control, I lift myself and slowly squeeze every inch of him as I do.

"Fuck yes," he pants, peppering kisses across my shoulder.

I pick up my pace, riding him until we're both on the edge.

"Come for me," he growls in my ear, and my pussy detonates.

He buries his face in my neck, and I cry out his name, riding the high our bodies and minds crave.

Trembling in the aftershocks of my pleasure, Luca pulls out from me, and I have to bite my lip to stifle the whimper that comes with the loss of him.

It's at that moment I realize just how screwed I am.

Because if I don't get my heart in check, I'm liable to fall in love with this man.

Or maybe I already have.

Chapter Twenty-Three

LUCA

The warm early morning sun peeking through the curtains wakes me up. Blinded, I blink a few times to orient myself and remember where I am.

Telluride.

Date with Leigh.

Gondola.

Coffee table.

Bedroom.

I roll over and check the other side of the bed to make sure it wasn't all a dream.

It wasn't.

God, she's beautiful when she sleeps. She's beautiful all the time, but seeing her like this—her blonde waves splayed across the pillow, and the morning light dancing from her bare shoulder down the curve of her body, half-covered with the thick, fluffy comforter—a knot forms in my throat at the idea of waking up every day to this. And I can't deny I'd do just about anything to make it a reality.

Last night was—

Rolling on to my back, I sigh and drag a tired hand over my face.

It was everything I could have hoped for and absolutely don't deserve.

Leigh stirs beside me and snuggles over into my side, chasing the warmth of my body like a fox burrowing into its den. She lets out a sleepy hum as she tangles her legs with mine and nestles into my chest.

Content to stay here all damn day—or at least until the guys decide they've had enough of babysitting—I wrap my arm around Leigh and hold her close.

Thirty blissful seconds are all I get before there's a knock at the guesthouse door.

So much for all day.

"Who is it?" Leigh mumbles sleepily. "Is it Zach?"

"I'll go see." I press a kiss to her forehead. "Even if it is, I've got him. You sleep."

She utters more unintelligible mumbles as she rolls away from me, burrowing into the blankets and drifting back to sleep.

It's a simple act. An indulgence she wouldn't have allowed herself a few days ago. It's progress. Hope.

With a pep in my step and hope in my heart, I make my way out into the living room, tugging on my jeans along with my sweater from last night.

The knocking starts again just as I reach the door.

"I'm coming, I'm coming," I mutter. As I tug it open, I find my twin with one hand raised and the other wrapped around a piping hot cup of coffee.

"Why the hell are there a shit ton of boxes being delivered at eight a.m. on Christmas Eve?" he asks, pushing past me into the kitchen to get out of the cold.

"Good morning to you too," I mumble, closing the door behind him.

When I turn around to follow, I see Enzo has stopped at the corner of the kitchen island, his eyes glued to where my boxer briefs and socks are strewn across the coffee table. "I take it things went well last night?"

"You could say that."

Enzo shakes his head and sets the cup of coffee—presumably for Leigh, considering neither of us drinks the stuff—down on the kitchen island. "I hope you know what you're doing."

"I do." There's a renewed confidence in my voice that wasn't there yesterday. And God does it feel good. Nothing can bring me down. Not today. Not when Leigh and I are finally in a good place.

Enzo raises a skeptical brow but doesn't push the subject. "And the boxes?"

"Oh, they're the presents for Zach that I had Carson pick up from Leigh's apartment in New York."

"All of them?" Accusatory disbelief laces his tone. "I just don't see Leigh going overboard like that on gifts. You, on the other hand…"

I shrug, rounding the kitchen counter to grab a cup and pour myself a glass of water. "Okay, so maybe I also bought him a few things."

"A few?"

"Okay, a lot of things," I admit, knowing damn well I'm never going to hear the end of it from Leigh. But I don't care. It's my first Christmas with Zach. I'm allowed to spoil the kid.

"Speaking of Zach." I glance in the direction of the main house. "Where is he?"

"He's in the main house drinking coffee and watching that male stripper movie with Holt." Enzo says it with such nonchalance that it's entirely impossible to tell if he's serious or not.

I slam down my glass and reach for my jacket, ready to make heads roll. "Fucking hell, Enzo. He's two."

My twin tips his head back and lets out a rough laugh. "God, what kind of uncle do you take me for?"

"The kind who has never been around a kid in his life."

"I resent that statement. I dated that one girl from back home who had a kid."

"You were going to marry her, Enzo, and it was a puppy, not a kid. And afterwards, you decided you were never dating anyone with an attachment to animals again."

"It was the same thing. She dressed the damn thing in clothes." Enzo huffs and eyes the bar cart in the corner, and I'm fairly certain if I keep down the avenue of the woman in question, he'll make his way over there and pour us doubles of the first alcohol he finds.

I shake my head and drop it. "What's Zach really doing?"

"He's dressed, has a fresh diaper, and is eating pancakes while watching *Scooby Doo* with Bash and Holt."

"The new one or the old one?"

"The old one, duh," Enzo scoffs, rolling his eyes. "Again, what kind of uncle do you take me for?"

A good one, but I'm not about to inflate his ego. He already knows I'd trust him with my life and that of my son.

My gaze softens as I connect with his, and we share a twin moment. "Thank you for taking care of him."

"You're welcome," he says with a tilt of his head. "You and Leigh deserved a night to…reconnect."

The way he says reconnect, like he's wary of it, has the hairs on the back of my neck raising. "You don't sound convinced."

"That's because I'm not sure if what I have in my pocket is going to make things better or worse."

"What is it?" I ask, eyes narrowed on his jacket.

Enzo reaches into his coat to the inner pocket and pulls out a folded-over envelope that is far too large to be a Christmas card.

Shit.

The moment I see it, I already know what it is. So much for nothing being able to bring me down today.

"They came in," I choke out, swallowing past the fear in my throat.

Enzo nods and extends the harbinger of my fate to me. "The guy who delivered the boxes gave it to me."

I eye the offending envelope and take it into my shaking hand. "Do the guys know they came?"

"Are you kidding? If they did, it'd already be opened, and you'd have both of them banging on your door, demanding answers one way or the other."

I nod and drop it onto the island like it burned me. "Do me a favor and don't tell them."

"Of course, but why?" Concern drips from his words, and I know his big logical brain is trying to figure out what the hell I'm playing at.

"Because I'm not going to look at them." I slide them back over to him. "In fact, can you take them and put them in my room?"

His eyes go round, and he looks down at the envelope and back up at me like I'm insane. "Are you serious?"

"Yeah. I think so." I give the wishy-washy answer for his benefit, so he doesn't sound the alarm and hold a family meeting to discuss my answer. But I'm confident in my answer.

"You don't want to know?"

I shake my head. "I don't need to know. I want this with Leigh either way, and Zach is amazing. Even if he's not mine, I'll raise him as my own."

"Fuck." Enzo runs a hand through his hair. It's the one thing we both do when we're caught off guard. "That's a lot to take on after one weekend."

"When you know, you know." I shrug and glance toward the room where Leigh is sound asleep. "They're it for me."

Enzo chews his lip for a moment. "All right." He nods. "You know I'll support you no matter what. So will the other two assholes."

"Thank you." How did I get so damn lucky to find these guys?

Enzo picks up the envelope and tucks it back into his coat. "But you gotta come get your son, because while you might have found your happily ever after, the guys want to hit the slopes and find a snow bunny or two."

I cock a scrupulous brow. "That include you?"

He barks a laugh. "Absolutely fucking not. Women are nothing but fucking trouble."

"I hope one day the right woman comes along and makes you eat your words."

"Single till the day I die."

A vise clamps a little tighter around my heart as I witness the hint of sadness in his gaze. "For your sake, I hope not."

My twin deserves his own happy ending. Maybe even more so than I do.

Chapter Twenty-Four

LEIGH

Today was a fairytale.

I never imagined I'd be saying that about anything surrounding Christmas, let alone Luca Donati, but here we are, making magic. I'll never forget the smile on Zach's face while decorating gingerbread cookies, or his giggles as we tobogganed down the small hill behind the guesthouse. Forever ingrained in my mind will be the taste of hot chocolate on Luca's lips and the sting of pain as he shoved me up against the pantry wall and made me come with just his fingers. Then his mouth on the kitchen island. And his cock as he bent me over the sofa.

There's never been a more productive nap time.

It's also the first time I've had a Christmas Eve where I didn't spend the majority of the day forcing a smile and pretending to be happy. Today, not a single one of my smiles has been involuntary.

Of course, all this sentimental bullshit could one hundred percent be the sex and tequila taking over and adding enchantment to my memories, where there is none.

But I don't think it is.

I think Telluride is magic. Or maybe it's Bucket List Christmas.

Okay, it's tequila.

In my defense, Holt pours them strong and, since they got back to the house, Bash has made sure none of us are without a drink in our hands. It's a terrible combination, but I don't hate it.

The twinkling lights of the tree catch my eye, and I trace the glittering tinsel-filled branches down to the piles of presents below that we just finished wrapping. They're all a mess—too much tape, uneven corners, and a few that don't have enough paper. So the guys added an extra misshapen piece to make it work.

Guy logic.

But still, they're perfect. And watching them play Santa, giggling with glee over how they think Zach will react, was worth it.

Zach is *absolutely* going to lose his mind tomorrow morning.

There's just one final touch needed.

I lug the bag of flour, a spray bottle, and a cookie sheet I found in the pantry over to the fireplace and carefully set it down on the hearth before bending over to untie my shoes.

"As much as I love this view, do I even want to know what you're doing?"

I look over my shoulder at where Luca stands, leaning against the doorframe of the living room.

It's not even fair how sexy this man is. Sure, he looks good in a suit, but those cashmere sweaters over a button-down and the way he makes them look casual just turns my insides to mush.

My eyes fall to his feet, and I grin. "Come over here. I need your shoes."

"My shoes?"

"Yeah." I turn back and pour the flour out on the cookie sheet. "Actually, do you think Bash's feet are bigger than yours? Where are the guys, anyway?"

They disappeared while I was gathering the things I needed for this endeavor.

"They're in the hot tub." Luca slides up behind me, resting his hips against mine before leaning over and nipping my shoulder. "And if you're about to make a comment about foot size and dick size, you should really think twice."

"Get your mind out of the gutter, Donati," I tease. "But now that you mention it, is there a correlation?"

"Absolutely. Which is why I can say with confidence, my feet are much larger than Bash's."

"Just give me your shoes." I roll my eyes.

He chuckles as he slips off his boots that probably cost more than my rent, and hands them to me.

"So what exactly are you doing?" He crosses his arms over his chest, watching me spray down the bottom of his shoe with water and push it into the mound of flour I formed on the baking sheet.

"I'm making Santa's footprints."

"What?"

I glance up and find he's wearing an expression that says he seriously has no idea what I'm talking about.

"Santa's footprints." Still no recognition, so I explain. "I'm going to use your boots to make it look like Santa walked across here, leaving snow from his boots as he put the presents under the tree and filled our stockings."

Luca's brows raise and my jaw drops, realizing just how far the deprivation goes when it comes to Donati parent involvement. "Your parents never did something like this?"

"That would be a no."

My smile falls a bit. "Mine did every year. Even after I knew the truth about Santa, they still made a show of it just to keep a little bit of magic."

Luca's eyes soften. "And now you get to share that with Zach."

"I—"

The sound of Luca's phone ringing cuts me off—a blaring horn that in any other situation I'd think signaled someone was stealing something.

He pulls it out of his pocket and mumbles an apology as he fumbles to silence it.

No image pops up on the Facetime call, but I immediately recognize the area code.

Shady Grove.

"Is it your family?" I whisper, praying it's just someone calling about his car's extended warranty.

Luca winces. "My mother."

My gut twists and not because of the person on the other end of the phone. It's the look of longing in Luca's eyes and the pain on his face. It's the look of a man who wishes things could've been different.

Which is why I find myself reassuring him. "You don't have to ignore it because of me."

"I'm not," he says, his eyes never leaving the phone screen. "She's been calling every day for the last month."

His admission floors me.

"If you need to answer it, I can go." I set down his boots and grab my own phone from the hearth.

"No," he blurts out. "Stay."

I hesitate, everything in me telling me to run and that this is a bad idea.

Again, maybe it's the lingering tequila, but I find myself nodding slowly. "If that's what you need."

He looks up at me, and nods once as he swipes the screen to answer.

"Oh, Luca," Isabella Donati croons in a sickly-sweet tone. "I am so happy you finally answered."

I glance from off camera at the visage of his mother. She's every bit the delicate socialite I remember. Not a single hair is out of place, and she's got more makeup on her Botox filled face than a clown at the circus.

"Hello, Mother." His voice is soft yet clipped, and tension radiates through his shoulders. "Merry Christmas."

"Well, it would be if all my children were under one roof."

God, she's insufferable.

Luca gives her an irritated scowl. "No 'hi, how are you?' Or 'what's new with you in the last ten years?' Just going to jump right in then with the insults."

Isabella scoffs, examining her immaculately manicured nails. "You know I've never been one to sugarcoat, dear."

"Unless it suits you."

"Oh, come now, Luca." She pouts. "Enough is enough. It's time you and Enzo come home. We have so much to celebrate. Your sister is pregnant, and that baby deserves to know their uncles."

Gianna's pregnant? The news shouldn't make my heart clench, but to think once upon a time I'd be the one she'd call to tell leaves me teetering between nostalgic and uneasy.

"Does Enzo know all this?" Luca deadpans.

"You've always been the more reasonable twin." It's a nonanswer if I've ever heard one.

"No, I've always been the one you could manipulate, but I haven't forgotten everything you said when you cut us off."

"Oh, don't be dramatic, Luca."

My strong, resilient twin shakes his head. "This was a mistake. I'd love it if we could all fix things, Mom, but you need to fix things with Enzo first, on your own, before you get to meet my family."

"Family?" This word instantly piques her interest. "You mean those boys you run around with instead of coming home to us?"

My body freezes, my mind racing with all the ways he could spin this while simultaneously praying that he's not going to do what I think he is.

We don't even know for sure he's Zach's father. Nor have we had any sort of conversation about what this is—if it's anything at all. I mean, I know it's something, but it doesn't have a title. It's definitely not, "Oh yeah, I'd love to tell your mom," let alone see her again after all these years. Because news flash, I don't want that. Ever. And not just me. There's not a chance in hell Zach is going anywhere near that witch of a woman.

"No, Mom," Luca doubles down. "I mean *my* family."

Fuck.

Fuck. Fuck. Fuck.

Isabella stills, her calculating blue eyes narrowing. "What the hell are you talking about, Luca?"

"You remember Leighton Bennet?"

Nope. This isn't happening. I'm not that girl anymore. I changed my name and made a life for myself. If he thinks I'm going to allow him to use Zach and me in some ass backwards way to stick it to her, he's got another think coming.

I will him to look at me. Glance in my direction. Anything so I can shut this shit down. But his eyes remain locked on his mother.

"The little thief who stole from me?"

My blood pressure skyrockets. That bitch. I have never hated that nickname more than I do when it slithers off her tongue.

"You know she didn't," Luca growls. "She and her son joined us this year for Christmas."

"Is this your way of telling me you're marrying her?"

"Not yet."

Whoa. Whoa. Whoa. Slow down, buddy. Anger and panic swirl like a category five hurricane in my chest. This is all moving faster than I'm comfortable with. *You might be my son's father, but as far as we go, we've fucked a few times. And while I really like you, I'm not ready to hear wedding bells.*

"Good," she seethes. "Because if you think my son is going to marry some trollop and take on her bastard son, you are gravely mistaken."

That does it. Luca snaps.

"Do you even hear yourself? For the love of God, the last ten years I have done nothing but hope someday you'd see reason. That you'd realize your views on what we should be is wrong and classist. We aren't the fucking Kennedy's. No one cares if I played baseball or that Enzo decided not to continue in the family business. What matters are the moments we share. And all the ones we've missed because you're too petty to see reason." Luca's chest heaves. "And he's not a bastard."

My world stops spinning.

"You got the results?" My whispered question is out before I can stop myself.

"Is she there?" Isabella shrieks.

"No," Luca says, refusing to look my way despite my desperation for any indication he knows who the father of my son is.

"I'm sorry you feel like our way of life is wrong," Isabella continues, her chin held high. "We raised you with higher standards. If you don't want to rise to meet them, then maybe this call was a mistake."

"Maybe it was." Luca sighs and there's no mistaking the defeat and sadness that haunts his voice. "Goodbye, Mom."

She doesn't bother responding, ending the call before Luca has the chance to.

"That was—I—" My spinning mind can't latch onto a single thought as I try to put into words what just happened. When it finally does, it's the one thing that's most important to me. "Did you get the results?"

"Yes," he whispers, still unwilling to look at me.

"Zach is yours?"

Luca's phone drops from his hand, hitting the floor with a thud. "I have no idea."

"What do you mean?"

He finally looks up at me, his big blue eyes glistening, and I can see his silent request to leave it written across his face. But there's no way in hell I can do that. Not after that phone call. Not after all the things he put out into the universe.

"I haven't looked at the results."

"But you just told your mom—"

"I know," he snaps and runs a hand through his hair, tugging on the strands like they are a lifeline. "But it doesn't matter if he's mine. I want you guys to be my family."

"Don't you think I should have gotten a say in that?" I throw my hands up before letting them fall in a desperate move for him to understand. "Luca, we just started whatever this is. You can't just give up a chance to fix things with your family without even knowing. Not only that, you're out here making insinuations that aren't true, and for what? To stick it to your mom? That's not how you get back in her good graces?"

"Is that what you think I was doing?" He takes a step toward me, and I immediately step back. "This is what I want."

"Do you hear how crazy that is?"

He falters, stopping mid stride. "Are you telling me you don't?"

"No, I—" Shit, I don't even know what I'm trying to say. "Four days together isn't enough. Especially if Zach isn't yours."

"You don't get it, do you?" His words drip with an almost deranged tone as he lifts his hands and gestures around the room. "This is all I need. Enzo, Bash, and Holt have been my family for the last ten years. You and Zach stumbling into our little tradition is the best thing that's happened to me. My family has been a clusterfuck for longer than I can remember. And as much as my mother thinks she's going to fix things overnight, there's not a chance in hell of that happening. I might not have known I wanted this before this week, but now I can't imagine my life without you. "

Tears threaten to fall, and I swallow hard to keep them in place. "It sounds like you've got it all figured out."

His eyes search mine, and I watch as they harden as he realizes he's not going to find what he's looking for.

"You don't want this."

It's not a question, and I'm left with the sinking feeling that I've just shattered every bridge we built.

I inhale a steadying breath and cross my arms over my chest, grasping my biceps for strength. "Luca. I barely just got over the fact that you are not the same guy I remember. How the hell am I supposed to make informed decisions about our future when I didn't even know it was an option last week…" My voice trails off, and I look him dead in the eye. "How can I decide if we don't even know if Zach is yours?"

"Does it matter?"

Does it?

I know what my heart wants me to say, but that's nothing more than the stuff of fairytales. So naturally, I push it down in a tiny little box and slap duct tape on that bitch.

The crux of it is I have to protect my son. I have to protect myself.

"Yes," I exhale, shattering my own heart as I do. "Because if he's not yours, you still have the option to fix things with your family."

He opens his mouth to counter, but I lift my hand to stop him.

"I know you say you don't want that, but if you could see your own face when you talk to your mother, you'd see what I do. Love and hope that someday you'll all find your way back to each other."

"Leigh—" he breathes.

"If Zach isn't yours, you don't have to keep playing house with us. You can walk away. I have to do what's best for Zach, and if you aren't his father, then I have to approach this differently. God, I've been so stupid. What if you decide in a month you don't want us? In a year? At that point, not only will you break my heart, you'll break his too. I can't do that to him."

"So what?" he spits, venom lacing his tone. "If Zach isn't mine, you're just going to live in a bubble and never let anyone love you?"

He loves me.

Is that what this is? It's been four days.

I push the absurd thought from the forefront to examine later. "Maybe this was a mistake."

"Don't do this, Leigh," he pleads.

"Open the results."

"No."

Desperation takes hold and I issue a plea of my own. "I need to know if he's yours."

So I can plan.

Wrap my head around our future.

"No."

A frustrated huff escapes me. "You stubborn—Luca. Please."

"Fine." His glare rips through me before he turns on his heel and exits the room. He's back in seconds, a large, folded envelope in his hand. "You can open them. I don't need a piece of paper to tell me what I already know."

And with that final sentiment, he tosses the results on the floor and storms from the room.

Chapter Twenty-Five

LUCA

So much for happy endings.

That singular thought has grown legs, procured a ten-inch blade, and is stabbing my heart—repeatedly.

I stumble out the door to where my best friends are all drinking beers, laughing in the hot tub. Silence washes over the deck as the door slams behind me, and they all swing their heads in my direction.

"Luca? Are you okay?"

I'm not sure which of them says it, but it doesn't matter, because no. I'm not okay. Nothing about me is okay.

I thought we were on the same page. Wanted the same things. In my mind, it was romantic—a grand gesture, if you will—telling off my mother and stating my intention to marry the woman who has consumed every fiber of my being. Isn't that what guys do in the romance books she reads? Wasn't that what she wanted?

Fuck, how did this go so wrong?

Crossing the deck in a haze, I swing my legs over the edge of the hot tub and splash down, not bothering to undress.

"What the fuck, Luca?" Bash yells.

"My thoughts exactly," I mutter.

"Where's Leigh?" Holt asks. "And why do you look like someone killed your dog right in front of you?"

"Inside. And because she did. Only replace dog with dreams of a future."

Enzo's eyes narrow. "Start from the beginning."

So I do.

Though I'm pretty sure I black out because I don't remember telling the story by the time I've finished. But I must've, because each of my friends is looking at me through the steam like they are ready to punch my teeth in.

The only one with a good excuse to do so is Enzo.

I don't think I've ever seen my twin look as homicidal as he does right now.

"That's a lot to unpack, but let's put a pin in the way you colossally fucked up with Leigh and talk about you and our *lovely* mother." Enzo's voice is melancholy with a hint of murder. "How long have you been talking to her?"

"Enzo, I—"

"How. Long. Luca." His words are staccato, taking over the knife and plunging where Leigh's rejection left off.

"She's been calling for the last month or so, but I didn't answer until tonight."

"Why the fuck would you do that?" he thunders, slamming his fist into the water, causing Bash and Holt to wince. "That woman has never done anything without an agenda."

"Gianna's pregnant."

"I don't give a flying fuck if she's the next Octomom. She chose to sit by and watch our parents silently ostracize us and picked up the slack when we wouldn't, so she could be the golden child."

"I'm sorry." I wince.

"I—" He runs his hand through his hair, slicking it back. "Fuck, I know you are. And I know you didn't do any of this because you wanted to hurt me. But you did. You know what they did to me. To us. And still, you can't help yourself when they dangle redemption in front of you."

"I told her no." And for the first time in a long time, it didn't hurt. Of course, that's when I thought my own dreams were still on the table.

Now I'm floating, searching for solid ground.

"This time." Enzo's jaw ticks. "You told her no this time. But what about next time? What about when you have a family of your own and they want to be a part of their grandchild's life?"

"It won't happen," I reassure him.

I'd need a family first. But that's not the point. He's right. Even though my track record has shown my loyalty, at the first opportunity, I broke.

"Even if it means your children will never know their grandparents?"

"We didn't know ours."

"And now you chase family like it's a goddamn sport."

"That's not what I'm doing."

"You sure about that?" Enzo presses. "Should I go ask Leigh?"

"Low fucking blow."

"He's right." Bash finally decides to jump into the fight, only I'm not sure whose side he's on until he continues. "Are you sure you aren't just projecting the way you cling to family onto Leigh?"

"No." My jaw clenches right alongside my fists. I inhale a steadying breath, so I don't give into the need to connect said fists with my best friend's jaw. "If this was just an idea, I could've found someone years ago. Trust me, plenty of women have tried. I didn't want it then, and I don't want it with anyone else now. Shit with Leigh is complicated, and usually I steer clear of that, but with her? I want it all. The white picket fence, or in this case maybe the upper east side apartment, and every messy moment it's going to take to get there."

Enzo sucks in a sharp breath. "You're going to move to New York?"

Our eyes connect. The same set of eyes on two different souls, and I know he feels my words when I say them. "I love her."

"Does she know this?" Holt asks.

"I mean," I scrub my hand down my face, recalling the conversation. "I just let our mother know I was going to marry her, so I think she knows."

My twin sighs but doesn't look away. "No, she knows you're a psycho stalker who might be the father of her child and wants to trap her in a marriage she didn't ask for. Do you see the problem here?"

Disappointment rocks my soul, and I look away first. "Fuck."

"You did it again," Bash huffs with a laugh.

"I did."

If this was anyone else other than my best friends, I might deny it, but they know me inside and out. Once again, I got ahead of myself. And as it does every time I do so with Leigh, it bit me in the ass.

"Did you give her the results?" Enzo whispers, but it's not soft enough that Bash and Holt don't hear.

"You got them?" Hurt flashes across Holt's face.

"Yes, on both accounts."

"How did you conveniently leave that part out?" Bash raises his voice and crosses his arms over his chest. "What did they say?"

"I don't know. I didn't look at them."

"Why the hell not?"

"Because like I told Leigh. It doesn't matter what's in that envelope. I'm all in."

Silence washes over the hot tub as Bash and Holt scrutinize my words. I watch as they go from anger to understanding, to acceptance, and finally back to brotherly love.

Bash is the first to break and lets out a long, slow whistle. "You really fucked this up, my dude."

I grunt. "Thanks, Captain Obvious."

"You really thought you were gonna win her over with that power move, didn't you?" Holt teases and even though I'm annoyed, I'm glad I have them in my corner.

"Clearly."

"So what are you going to do now?" Bash asks. For as much as the guy hates being involved in planning, when it comes to drama, he's the first to jump in.

I shake my head in defeat. "I have no fucking idea."

"Lucky for you I'm the king of smooth moves."

Enzo huffs a laugh. "And on that note, I'm going to get us more drinks so we can all forget later about Bash's smooth moves."

My twin hops up, slides out of the hot tub, and makes a break for the warmth of the main house. I can't help but wonder if he's going to see Leigh. Is she still in the living room making those stupidly adorable footprints? Is she already planning her escape?

Shit.

Am I going to wake up to find both of them gone?

Panic grips my spine, and I suck in a ragged breath.

"Don't listen to him," Bash scoffs. "We'll come up with something that's going to knock her off her feet."

Will we? Is that what it's going to take? I thought that's what I already did? Maybe I really don't know anything about her.

No.

That's not it.

I know plenty. Leigh's a romantic, but she doesn't wear her heart on her sleeve. She puts Zach first. Always. Never herself.

Damn it.

I really did fuck up.

"No," I whisper.

"What do you mean, no?"

"That's where I went wrong." God, it all seems so clear now. "Leigh doesn't need grand gestures. She doesn't need fancy words or shiny things."

"What does she need?"

"Action. Stability. Someone who isn't going to run."

"Didn't you already tell her you aren't?"

The answer was there the whole time, but instead of listening, I did what I would have wanted.

Shit. I'm the chick in this relationship. I want the grand gestures. Leigh though—she wants the silent action. The quality time. The acts of service. She needs to know I'm not going anywhere, and that she and Zach can count on me.

"Yeah," I agree, a hint of a plan starting to form. "I know what I need to do."

Chapter Twenty-Six

LEIGH

Why does it feel like I'm the villain in my own story?

This is what I wanted.

Right?

I finger the soft envelope, setting it down on the kitchen island—unopened—I pick up my phone and call Willow for the tenth time.

When she doesn't answer, I try Indie. Only to end with the same result.

Sure, it's three a.m. on Christmas Eve on the east coast. But don't they know emotional panic has no time constraints, and I need them to confirm that I'm not insane? That my concerns are valid. That I didn't go and ruin my chances for a beautiful, amazing thing because I'm freaking the fuck out.

Luca's words haunt me.

Are you just going to live in a bubble and never let anyone love you?

Is that what I'm doing?

No.

I let people love me. Willow and Indie love me. The guys on the Renegades love me and Zach.

I can practically hear Luca's mocking laugh. *You know those aren't the same.*

Damn it.

I hate it when he's right. Especially when he's still wrong.

He might've thought he was choosing Zach and me with that stunt, but it was just a giant middle finger to his mother. What did he think? That I'd jump into his lap and *say take me I'm yours* because he said he wants to marry me, so Zach and I can be his family?

Maybe to other girls that would be romantic, but all I can think is, how the hell does that even work? Is wanting this enough? I'm in New York and he's in California. He's got a team, while I've got a whole philanthropy to run. Can we even make it outside the bubble of Telluride? Because that's what this is—a bubble waiting to pop.

That's why I need to know who Zach's father is.

Right?

Logic has never failed me and yet that feels like the wrong answer. Not that the other guy is going to show up and be a problem. I don't even know his last name. But should he ever show up again, or find Zach in ten years through a DNA test, will Luca be okay with sharing the role of dad? Has he even considered these kinds of things?

With his jump-without-a-parachute track record, I'm guessing that's a hard no.

And those are just questions when it comes to Zach.

What about just normal, everyday relationship questions? Like, does he want more kids? Because I'm not sure I do. Or is he a dog person or a cat person? Because there is no way in hell I'm getting a fucking cat.

Closing my eyes, I pinch the bridge of my nose. When did this all get so damn complicated?

Oh, that's right. When I decided to hate-fuck a guy against a vending machine.

The back door jiggles and opens, and while I don't bother looking to see who it is, I pray it's not Luca.

"You look as shitty as he does."

Enzo.

I recognize the deep voice, the same as his twin. Except with Luca, there's a warmth that Enzo lacks.

"Not tonight, Enzo," I sigh, tears stinging the corners of my eyes.

I listen to his footsteps as he rounds the counter to the beverage fridge built into the island. "You sure? We could toast to my brother being an asshat."

A sound that is more sob and less chuckle escapes me, and I glance up to see him lifting a bottle of beer in my direction.

At least it's not tequila.

"I should go," I whisper. I'm not entirely sure where. Zach is sleeping in the main house, but the idea of being one wall away from Luca sounds like a special brand of torture. And with the guys in the hot tub, it's not like I can escape to the guesthouse, even just for a bit.

"Please don't." Enzo rounds the island, setting down a beer for each of us before sliding into the seat next to me.

My gaze narrows and I shake my head. "What is it with you Donati boys thinking you can demand things, and everyone will just fall into line?"

"You've met our mother." He shrugs.

"Fucking witch."

Enzo lifts his beer. "Amen."

"What do you want, Enzo?"

He brings the bottle to his lips and takes a long pull before he answers. "To convince you to give my brother a chance."

I arch a brow, and study the chaos twin in front of me, uncertain if he's doing this for the plot or he really means it. "If only it were that simple."

"Isn't it?" he presses. "Anyone with two eyes can see that you guys are crazy about each other."

"It's been four days." I cling to logic, knowing this couldn't truly be what everyone sees.

"And?"

"He told your mom he's going to marry me."

"And maybe he will someday."

"He can't just go telling people that."

"Have you met my brother?" Enzo tips his head and laughs. "On our first day of little league, he told the coach that he was going to play in the MLB one day."

"Enzo."

"Listen." He spins in his chair to face me, blue eyes so similar to his brothers lock on mine. "I'm not saying he's not a pretentious dreamer. In the span of a week, the asshole tricked you into showing up in Telluride, and thought he could go toe to toe with Isabella Donati and come out with everything he's ever wanted. He's delusional on his best days. But that's why we love him. He does these things with the best intentions. He can't help himself. He wants to see the good in people and situations. He chases it like a fucking hound chases a fox. But it's never with the intention of eating the fox. He'd sooner snuggle the shit out of it and make it his pet."

"And that makes me the pet?"

"No." He takes another long drink, and I lean forward in my chair, waiting to see if he's going to explain what the hell he means.

Enzo sets down the bottle and stands. Looking down at me, he finally puts me out of my misery. "You're his reason. Without you, he wouldn't have realized our family was fucked all those years ago. Without you, he wouldn't have had the heart to allow Jack to bring us all together. And without you, he wouldn't've dared to dream a family was even possible for him. So while it might seem fast for you, for Luca this has been years in the making."

My jaw drops as he silently rounds the island and grabs another four beers from the fridge. He heads for the door but pauses just before he walks through.

"The dumbass can't do anything without jumping in with both feet. So good luck training that out of him if you decide he's worth it. And for the record, I hope you do. I rather enjoy being an uncle."

I watch as he leaves, staring at the door long after he's gone.

I'm Luca's reason.

And he's…

The first thought that comes to mind sends me into a fit of laughter.

He's my wrecking ball.

Luca jumping in with both feet is probably the only reason we are where we are. He wasn't afraid of my walls or my logic. He came at them and with love and persistence, chipping away at them swing after swing with his never-ending positivity.

With this new perspective, it's almost sweet.

Almost.

But it doesn't completely wash away the fear coiled deep in my belly that someday he's going to realize it could be easier with someone else.

I can't offer him the promise of marriage someday, but maybe if he's willing to meet me halfway and allow me to logic where he jumps, I can offer him one day—one moment—at a time.

My eyes fall on the results in front of me.

Tomorrow might just be a Merry Christmas after all.

Chapter Twenty-Seven

LEIGH

Snow gently falls outside, blanketing the ground in a fresh layer of white.

It's the perfect Christmas morning aesthetic. Paired with Zach snuggling into my side after I pulled him into bed with me last night, it couldn't be more perfect. Well, mostly—but hopefully that will change. If I don't let my anxiety and fear get the best of me.

I glance down at Zach, memorizing for the millionth time his long lashes and tiny button nose. I've missed these moments the last few days. Though I can't deny it's been nice to have the help or that seeing Zach smile with the boys has made my heart burst.

Still, these moments where it's just the two of us will always be my favorite.

He begins to stir, stretching his little limbs out like a starfish, signaling my moment of peace is coming to an end.

"Merry Christmas, sweet boy." I press a kiss to his forehead, and he beams up at me with a lazy, toothy grin.

"Mewy Chwistmas," he yawns.

I smile right back at him, knowing he's been working with Bash and Enzo to say those two words for the last few days.

"You ready to go see what Santa brought you?"

"Santa!" he mimics loudly, though I'm not sure he completely understands, but he understands the "go" and it's clear he is more than ready.

After changing him and slipping myself into a set of appropriate flannel pajamas, we make the long walk from the bedrooms to the main living room.

The smell of coffee wraps me in a warm hug, and I tell myself no matter what happens, at least there's a hot cup of coffee to feed my soul or catch my tears. Either way, this morning is about Zach.

Practically bouncing with each step, Zach tugs my hand forcefully, mumbling the names of Luca and his best friends in excitement.

I just hope the four of them share the same sentiment. There's no way of knowing what I'm going to walk in on, if the guys are even awake yet. I considered going to find Luca last night to talk, but figured it would be best to let us each have the night to process. God knows I needed it. With the sun came more clarity—and anxiety—but also a weird sort of anxious peace.

It's an oxymoron, I know, but that's the best way I can describe it. Logically, I know everything is still a clusterfuck, but at the same time, my heart and mind know I can't keep hiding behind these walls.

Thankfully, I know Luca won't let me. I just need to see if he'll meet me halfway.

I hope he'll meet me halfway.

When we enter the living room, my eyes stay glued on Zach. He stops in his tracks, his eyes going wide with wonder.

"Wooow," he gasps with all the innocence of a child, and I wish I could bottle the moment and keep it forever to remember what the magic of Christmas looks like.

Zach takes off running, and I follow his movements across the room, stopping first at the stockings overflowing with tiny toys and presents, next to a giant play Range Rover that Luca insisted he needed. From there, he follows the Santa footprints to the tree, stepping in each of them as he goes. I can't help but let my thoughts drift, knowing they're Luca's footprints—and if he grows up to have even half that man's heart, the world will be a better place. Finally, Zach turns and runs over to the couch, jumping into the space between Luca and Enzo. Bash and Holt sit on the opposite side of the sectional.

I didn't even realize they were in the room, all of them sitting like silent statues as they watch my son.

Luca sweeps Zach into his arms and wishes him a Merry Christmas, which Zach excitedly returns before pulling away and greeting each one of his uncles in the same manner.

As he does, Luca stands and grabs a steaming mug from the coffee table and closes the space between us. Dressed in a navy blue robe over a pair of flannel pants, with scruff and unkept hair, he looks every bit the role of Dad on Christmas morning. He's even got on fuzzy slippers to complete the ensemble.

My breath catches in my throat as he hands me the coffee, my fingers brushing his, and leans in to press a kiss to my forehead. I feel the ease of it course through my body all the way to my toes.

Cautiously, I pull back to search his eyes for any indication of where he's at—where we're at.

"Merry Christmas, Leigh."

Leigh.

Not Little Thief.

There was a time he called me that out of anger. And then once I knew the true meaning, it was out of adoration. But my name? It lacks both, leaving me with nothing to go on.

"Merry Christmas," I whisper.

His lips curve up, a good sign we're not about to have a fight and ruin Christmas morning. He takes a step back and extends his arm, offering for me to pass him and join the group.

"Now that the guest of honor is here"—his eyes dart to where Zach is snuggling in Enzo's lap—"let's get Christmas morning started."

I clench my jaw to keep it from dropping.

That's it?

That's all I get?

No explanation. No fight. No demands.

Just a kiss on the forehead and we're moving on?

"Leigh? Are you coming?" Luca's voice pulls me back, and my eyes track to where he's now sitting on the floor, playing Santa and handing everyone their stockings.

Dumbfounded as to what the hell is going on, I nod and pad across the short distance and sit across from him. Zach races from the couch to my lap and tears into the stocking Luca hands him, holding up each toy for me to examine and tossing aside the new toothbrush I made sure was in there for him.

"Just go with it," Luca whispers. "There'll be time to make sense of everything later."

I nod silently, not because I don't have anything to say—because trust me, there is so much I want to say to this man—but because I'm afraid if I speak, a sob will be the first thing that comes out.

Swallowing hard, I blink away my tears, watching as Zach finishes with his stocking and moves on to examining his new Range Rover.

It's the first year he's old enough to start getting into the excitement of Christmas morning and instead of fighting with me or demanding we figure things out, Luca is giving me—us—the gift of experiencing it without any of the weight of paternity, relationships, or what comes next.

Don't get me wrong, I still feel it in every smile Luca gives me and the longing side glances he gives Zach when he thinks none of us are looking.

We spend the morning laughing and smiling as we watch Zach shred open gift after gift. So many that I'm not sure how the heck we're going to get them all back to New York. Luca assures me it won't be a problem, but I'm more worried about where I'm going to house them.

Bash disappears only to return with fresh baked cinnamon rolls, and of course, a mimosa flight—with orange, cranberry and pineapple juices as options—for each of us. Because according to him, it's not Christmas without champagne to celebrate. He's even got sparkling cider for Zach in a sippy cup champagne flute.

By the time we're done with gifts and breakfast, we're well lubricated enough that Enzo, Holt, and Bash provide us with entertainment, singing *We Wish You a Merry Christmas*, but with each of them only singing one word at a time. They only make it through one verse before they start making up the words, and by the end of the second, we're all laughing too hard to continue.

It's perfect.

Every fucking moment of it.

And I've never been so sure this is where we're meant to be.

I silently get up and whisper in Enzo's ear, watching as a knowing smile tips his lips. He nods and stands from the couch, tipping his head at Holt and Bash before he goes and crouches in front of Zach. "Hey little man, want to go outside and see how fast the car can drive in the snow?"

"Enzo," Luca warns.

"Just on the deck, Enzo," I reiterate.

"So we can't see if it fits in a gondola and go cruise the main strip for ladies?" Holt asks, already up and tugging a coat over his pajamas.

"Not this time. Maybe after his nap."

"Deal," Bash agrees, slipping his shoes on.

The three of them grab my son and make themselves scarce, leaving me alone with Luca.

I spin around to where he's sitting on the edge of the sofa, eyeing me suspiciously. "If I didn't know any better, I'd say you're trying to get me alone."

I resist the urge to slide up between his legs and run my hands through his hair. Talking first. There will be time for that later. Hopefully. I told Enzo I needed at least an hour.

Crossing the room, I slip behind the tree and pull out the envelope I'd nestled in the branches last night.

Luca's shoulders tense the moment he realizes what's in my hands, but he doesn't say anything, only watches intently as I stop in front of the fireplace.

I glance down one last time and find exactly zero doubt in my heart when it comes to what I hold in my hands. When I look back up, my eyes track every inch of Luca's face, and I can't wait to calm the anxiety in his features.

"Let me start by saying thank you."

"You know what that phrase does to me." There's a hint of hope in his tone, and it only reminds me that this man is the exact opposite of me. Which is why he's exactly what I need.

"I know." I smile playfully. "And I hope I get to make you hard by uttering them for a very long time."

"Leigh." Luca exhales, his hope wavering. "What are you saying? Because I'm on edge here and I don't know what I'm allowed to say."

"I'm saying I was wrong."

He raises a brow. "Come again?"

Holding steady eye contact, the same way he does when he wants to make sure I'm listening, I inhale a long breath. "I was wrong last night for demanding you look at these." I lift the envelope, noting the way he frowns. "I was afraid. None of this is what I planned. I didn't come here expecting to find a family. I wanted to make sure you knew you might have a son and get our work done in time to get home for Christmas. But then you were…you. Frustratingly sweet, annoyingly persistent, and totally fuckable."

His wicked grin makes an appearance. "I'm going to add those to my resume."

"Of course you are," I huff, rolling my eyes.

"But if we're admitting faults, I was wrong too." Luca stands and closes the distance between us in four swift steps. "I shouldn't have gotten ahead of myself. You aren't one to jump five steps ahead without a fifteen-point plan and a list of to dos. I won't take it back because, if you'll have me, I fully intend on marrying the shit out of you. But I promise I'll try to look before I leap."

I open my mouth to protest his proposal, as this is exactly what scares me, but Luca continues.

"Calm that pretty little mind of yours. I mean someday, Leigh. Not today. Not tomorrow. But someday, if you'll have me, the offer will always be there." He reaches down and takes the hand not holding the results, intertwining it in his. "The question is, Leigh, what do you want? Because I've already told you, I don't need those." He dips his head toward the envelope.

"Neither do I."

His lips part, and he does his best to hide his shock. "Don't fuck with me, Little Thief."

"I'm not." And to prove it, I turn around and toss the unopened results into the fire.

The moment they are engulfed in flames, Luca wraps me in his arms. I chuckle against his chest before pulling back and bracketing his jaw with my hand. "You knocked down all my walls with those big ass feet of yours, and I'm glad you did. I'm still terrified we're moving too fast, but there isn't anyone else I can imagine sharing moments like these with. Zach loves you, and he deserves the world. A paternity test won't give him that. You will."

Tears fall freely down his face, and I wipe them away with my thumb.

"And what about you, Leigh?" His lip quivers. "Are you saying you love me too?"

I smirk, "I'm saying if you're a good boy, I'd be willing to tolerate you for the foreseeable future."

"Close enough," he chuckles and slants his lips over mine. But before he presses against me, he stops. "For the record, I love you too."

He loves me.

And even though I didn't say it out loud, I think I love him too.

Luca threads his fingers through my hair at the same time his hand grips my hip, pulling gently with both, so there is no part of us not touching.

It's as if we are two lost puzzle pieces, finally figuring out how to fit together. It's magical.

He lets out a gruff moan of relief and I part my mouth, delving into his to deepen our kiss. Slow and measured, we explore each other until I'm not sure where he ends, and I begin.

And I get the feeling maybe that's the way we're supposed to be.

He pulls away, only slightly, and smiles. "We should go out, so you don't miss seeing Zach in his new whip."

"Are you sure?" I run my hand up his chest, gently grazing the bars in his nipples. "As much as I want to see a toddler driving a Range Rover, Enzo promised me an entire hour for us to kiss and make up. And I might have a matching set of those panties you liked so much in red."

"As enticing as that sounds," he says, tilting his hips so his already hardening cock presses against my core, "and believe me, it's enticing as shit, but I plan on kissing you under the mistletoe for years to come. Let's go spend this first Christmas with our family."

Our family.

The fear that once consumed me, that I would lose Zach and end up alone for the rest of my days, melts away under his blue-eyed gaze.

Because while people leave us—through death or of their own

volition—some people stay, and that's what I'm choosing to hold on to.

I look up at Luca and smile, content and at peace. "Thank you for bringing back the magic of Christmas."

"Fuck," he groans. "And then you had to go and thank me."

"I'm just saying, I think our family can wait long enough for you to bend me over the couch real quick."

Luca groans again and buries his face in the crook of my neck. "Are you sure you won't marry me?"

I give a coy chuckle. "Not today."

He pulls back and smiles, pressing his forehead to mine. "But you're saying there's a chance?"

God, I love this man's unwavering hope.

"Make me come and I'll consider it."

Luca's hands cup my ass and lifts my legs, locking them around his hips. In four long strides, we're at the sofa. He tosses me down, drops to his knees, and hooks his fingers in the waistband of my pajamas.

"I'll make you come every day for the rest of my life if it means I get to keep you."

And then kisses me under the mistletoe.

Epilogue

LUCA

Thirteen months later

"We're going to be late," Leigh hollers from the front of our New York apartment, and I can picture her looking out the floor-to-ceiling windows in the living room down at the traffic below, pretending like her anxiety isn't getting the best of her.

She might claim to be a New Yorker at heart, loving the hustle and bustle of the city, but the more she splits her time in Los Angeles, the more I think she likes the slower pace.

Not that traffic isn't horrendous there too. It is. But it's easy to forget when you're standing on our balcony looking at the sunset over the Pacific Ocean.

I huff a laugh and yell back, "Tell that to Zach. He can't decide if he wants to wear the blue shirt or the purple one."

"Tell him it won't matter if we don't hurry up."

As if that's going to work. Shaking my head, I lean against the doorframe of Zach's room where he, in all his newly turned three-year-old glory, is standing naked from the waist up, hands on his hips, looking at the two shirts on the bed.

He gets this from me. How many times has he found me in the exact same position, getting ready for work in the morning? Usually, I'd find it adorable as shit, but today's a big day, and I need him to just pick a damn shirt.

I cross the room and kneel beside him. "What if you wear the purple one to see the judge, and then you can wear the blue one when we go out to dinner with your aunts and uncles?"

"Zo?"

"Yes, Enzo will be there."

"Hote?"

"Yup and Holt too."

"Bash Bash."

I chuckle, realizing we are going to have to name every single one of his aunts and uncles who are flying in for this special day. "Yes, Bash too."

"Dee?"

"And Indie."

"Low and Shop?"

"Yes, Willow and Bishop too."

Zach's brow furrows as he considers my offer. As much as I'd like to claim the trait as mine, this one's all Leigh. He carefully looks back and forth between the two button-down shirts and then smiles up at me. "Okay."

If only I'd come up with this solution ten minutes ago, we wouldn't be on the verge of running late. I'm fairly certain the court of law waits for no one, and today has been months in the making, so there's not a chance in hell I'm going to allow us to miss our scheduled appearance.

Throwing the blue shirt over my shoulder to take with us, I help Zach slide the shirt on and do up the buttons, silently thanking the Patron Saint of Toddlers that he didn't fight me on trying to do them himself. Now I just need the saint of traffic to help us get to the courthouse on time, so Leigh doesn't have a conniption.

The last thing I need is for her to be angry today. Not with everything

I have planned.

I look down at my sweet, confident, and brave boy. "You ready, buddy?"

Zach beams up at me. "Family Day, Dada!"

"Yeah, bud." I smile, blinking back the tears I promised Leigh wouldn't fall before the judge bangs her gavel. "Today *is* family day."

Traffic is a nightmare, but somehow, we make it with time to spare. *Thanks, traffic saint.*

Just as we're pulling up, Leigh reaches across Zach's car seat, offering me her open palm. "You nervous?"

I place my palm in hers and give a gentle squeeze. "Not even a little."

Leigh lets out a small laugh. Today is the day I get everything I've ever wanted. Starting with Zach officially becoming my son.

Six months after Telluride, on my birthday, Leigh asked me again if I wanted to know if I was Zach's biological father. Of course, I told her no. I still stand firm that it didn't matter. But then she followed up with, "If we do the test, then we'll know which form we need to file in order for you to formally become his dad."

The way my heart stopped.

This was better than saying she'd marry me.

Which I'm still hoping she will.

Very soon.

But going through with it meant confirming what I already suspected as I continued to spend time with Zach.

He isn't mine. At least biologically.

His nose is that of a stranger, and as he grows, he's got a little chin dimple that doesn't come from either Leigh's or my family.

But what he does have is my stubborn streak and a penchant for mischief. He's got my love of spicy food, and a capacity for compassion I take pride in instilling within him. That little boy is mine in every way that counts, and I am proud to call him my son.

Today just makes it official.

Zach places his hands around our entwined fingers and giggles, melting my heart like he somehow manages to do every single day.

How could I be nervous when this is everything I've wanted ever since the two of them stepped off that plane in Telluride?

"Cuttin' it close, don't you think?" Enzo says as he opens the door of the Escalade and offers a hand to Leigh.

"Your nephew is as bad as your brother when it comes to choosing an outfit, otherwise we would have been here twenty minutes ago."

Unbuckling Zach, I help him slide out of the car behind his mother. I follow after, rounding the back of the car to meet them.

Enzo laughs. "Well, you're here now. And I've got some exciting news."

I cock a brow. "What's that?"

When Enzo says he has good news, it's fifty-fifty if it's actually good or something he perceives as interesting, like, the stock market being up X number of points.

He smirks, like he knows I'm silently judging him. It's twin telepathy at its finest.

"We know where we're going next year for Bucket List Christmas."

"Holt finally picked?" I ask, knowing he was struggling between two locations. Not that he would allow the rest of us any input. It's become somewhat of a pride thing for all of us to take the time to consider what Jack would want for that particular year in our lives.

"Yeah." Enzo pauses for dramatic effect. "Ultimately, surfing won."

Leigh rolls her eyes dramatically.

"I know, shocker." Over the last year, Holt took up surfing as a hobby, since it was something Jack loved. I should have known that would have played into his pick.

"So where are we going?" Leigh asks.

"Cozumel, Mexico, to visit the reef."

Shit.

I'm going to fucking kill Holt.

My eyes dart to my sweet, nerdy twin to see if he has any idea The Reef isn't referring to the coral in the ocean, but rather a high-end sex club where you can explore every kink imaginable under the light of the moon. But there's nothing. Not a trace of a knowing grin.

And it's my job this year to plan all the excursions.

I silently debate if I should let him in on the secret. Then again, maybe he'll find himself a little romance, or at the very least find someone to help him loosen the giant stick he's had lodged in his ass since our grandfather passed away a few months back.

No, I think I'm going to keep this bit of info to myself.

"After two years in the snow for Christmas, I can get behind coming home with a tan," Leigh says before grabbing Zach's hand. Spotting Indie, Willow, and Bishop waiting for us at the top of steps, she waves.

I watch her go, admiring the way the new coat I got her for Christmas hugs the curve of her waist and shapes her ass perfectly.

My twin leans over and nudges my shoulder. "Don't worry, I already looked into booking you the honeymoon bungalow for at least two nights."

Whipping my head to face him, I speak in a harsh whisper, "She hasn't said yes."

"Oh, come on. As if that woman is going to say no. You guys haven't been able to keep your hands off each other all year. And I'm pretty sure we all heard what that led to in Zermatt."

I bark a laugh. "It's not my fault you booked us a house that had all the rooms right next to each other."

"Never again."

"You're an ass."

"And you love me."

"I do."

I can't imagine the last year without him or the guys. We might not all live together, but they've always been a phone call away—of which I've had to utilize plenty of time when I stick my foot in my mouth— and they've gone out of their way to stop and see Leigh, Zach, and me whenever our schedules line up in LA or New York.

"You ready for this?" my twin asks, and I know it's not from a place of doubt, but love.

"Today can literally be penciled in as the best day of my life."

I haven't stopped smiling since the judge banged her gavel and officially named us the James family.

Leigh was shocked as hell by that, and she'll be even more shocked when she realizes I took the liberty of changing my last name. We won't have to change it later when she makes me the happiest man in the world again today.

It might be me jumping in with both feet, but I have the feeling my odds are pretty good.

Looking down the table in the tiny back room of our favorite Italian restaurant, I'm surprised we all fit.

In addition to the Bucket List Boys—as Leigh calls us—Indie, Willow, and Bishop, a handful of the Renegades we've become close with, and their manager, Graham, all came to celebrate with us.

And celebrate we have, especially Zach, who has gone up to every person and told them confidently, "We a family."

I reach over Zach, who is sitting between me and his mom, and run my fingers over her exposed collarbone.

She looks over at me, and nerves instantly take over and I feel my body tense.

"You okay?"

"Never better." I breathe, shifting in my seat so the weight of the ring box in my pocket isn't evident against my thigh.

Zach looks up, watching our interaction. "Momma, now you marry Dada"

Heat fills Leigh's cheeks. "Oh, sweet boy, no. We explained to you, that's not what today was about."

"No," Zach protests. And I give him a look that says *now is not the time*. After dessert is the time. We haven't even gotten our meals yet. But try telling that to a three-year-old.

"Dada," he continues, looking up at me with those big blue eyes that I can never say no to. "Momma's ring."

"Yeah," Bash chimes in from across the table. "When are you going to put a ring on it and make an honest woman out of our Baby Momma here?"

The fucking asshole knows exactly when.

"My Baby Momma," I growl.

Leigh glances from Bash to Zach, then back up at me.

I exhale and shrug my shoulders.

I stand from the table and take Zach's hand, helping him from his chair before offering my hand to Leigh.

"What are you doing?" Her voice is shaky, but not angry, so at least we're off to a good start.

When I give a slight tug, she rises to her full height.

The room goes silent.

I glance down at Zach and give him a smile. "Just like we practiced."

He smiles and nods.

Willow gasps and Indie cheers alongside Bash and Holt as I pull out the velvet box from my pocket. I fall to one knee in front of Leigh, followed by a collective round of "awws" as Zach does the same thing beside me.

"Leighton Renee Bennett James," I begin.

"Momma," Zach says at my side.

"I have wanted to ask you this question since Christmas morning in Telluride, but I knew you weren't ready to answer. Where I jump into the pool recklessly, you dip your toe in and make sure you aren't going to freeze. We've spent that last year warming up to one another. Learning to honor each other's quirks and communicate. You are my best friend—"

"Hey!" Bash and Holt exclaim in unison, and I shoot a pointed glare at them, which earns me a wary chuckle from Leigh.

I turn back to her, looking up into her tear-filled eyes. "As I was saying, you're my best friend, and the person I want to spend the rest of my life with. I love you, and even though you've already made me the happiest man on earth by allowing me to become the father of our son today, would you do me the honor of adding husband to my list of titles and letting me call you my wife?"

I glance over at Zach, who is smiling at Leigh, and give him a little nudge. "Now, bud."

"Mommy, will you marry Daddy?"

The longest split second of my life passes before Leigh huffs a choked laugh and smiles.

Her eyes leave Zach's and connect with mine. "I guess I could tolerate you for the rest of my life."

"That's not a yes."

Leigh rolls her eyes, the same way she did in Telluride. "Yes, I'll marry you."

I open the box, showing Leigh the ring I had Willow help me track down a few months back.

She gasps. "It's my mother's ring."

"I had help getting it." I throw a glance over at Willow, who played a fundamental part in stealing the ring from the tiny safe Leigh kept it in. "I knew you'd want her to be a part of this."

"Thank you," she says with a knowing smile.

A shiver runs down my spine and I force myself to ignore the twitch in my dick as I slip the ring onto her finger. It's a perfect fit.

I tug her down onto my knee and pull her and Zach against me as our friends and chosen family cheer around us, but I'm too busy savoring the feeling of having everything I've ever dreamt of in my arms.

"I love you, Luca," Leigh whispers against my ear.

"I love you too, my Little Thief."

THE END

Thank you so much for reading TINSEL IN TELLURIDE!! I really hope you loved Leigh and Luca's journey as much as I did writing it.

Need more of this incredible group of guys? Keep an eye out on my socials or join my NEWSLETTER to stay up to date! The next installment of Bucket List Christmas will release Christmas 2025!!

I appreciate each and every one of you for taking this journey with me. As an Indie Author, I would love your help spreading the word about TINSEL IN TELLURIDE. If you enjoyed the story, please consider leaving a review on Amazon, Goodreads, or even referring it to a friend.

Even a sentence or two makes a huge difference.
Thank you for taking this journey with me.

xoxo
Hayden

ALSO BY HAYDEN LOCKE

THE DRAFT SERIES

Midnight Renegade

Renegade Ruin

Renegade Rift - COMING SOON

LOVE IN ASPEN

Finally Home

ALSO BY HAYDEN LOCKE
WRITING AS K.M. RIVES

THE CULLING SERIES

The Replacement

The Indentded

Hybrid Moon Rising

The United

ACKNOWLEDGEMENTS

There was a time I wasn't sure this book was ever going to get written. I didn't know if it was a hairbrained idea to write a holiday series with team owners who it was very possible no one would care about.

Boy was I wrong!

From the moment readers read Luca and Leigh they were clamouring to find out their story. And I was more than ready to tell it. So when other characters started to get difficult to work with, I knew it was time for Luca and Leigh to shine.

But this story wasn't a one man show. Far from it. There have been so many people who have helped me on this whirlwind journey to get the words on the page.

To my husband—my rock, my home. Thank you from the bottom of my heart. You allow me to dream big and make them a reality. You never stop cheering me on—helping me plot through any holes that pop up and bringing me Dr. Pepper and Payday's when I need sustenance. Your fresh perspective and knowledge of the male orgasm is forever and always appreciated!

To my daughters—Thank you for always reminding me everyone needs a break for cuddles and board games. You guys are my world. #betheromance

To Elle Parker—I have no words. You are the friend, coworker and cheerleader I never knew I needed. This book would never have come to life without you and our daily work calls. You meet my anxiety with your own, bask in our shared type A greatness and together we manage to turn our shitstorm into beautiful words. It's a true artform, really. Thank you for being my dude. #LangstonForever

To Rachel—my fearless editor and friend. I am admittedly shit with commas but you'd never know it looking at this book. You made this story shine in every way possible! Thank you for knowing I work better under a deadline and having the grace to meet me there. Thank you for believing in me, listening to every hair brain idea and for loving em dashes as much as I do.

To Linds: You deserve all the praise in the world. It takes a truly incredible artist to take a vision and make it come alive on the page. And you do it, EVERY. SINGLE. TIME. I come to you with a plan. Thank you for giving life to Leigh and Luca in a way that is fun, loveable and truly freaking beautiful.

To Tehia—my penguin with a parachute—From the moment we met you believed in me with the force of a damn hurricane and you made sure I never forgot what a beautiful badass I am. Thank you for being my sounding board, my cheerleader but most of all thank you for being my friend.

To Marissa and Sam—thank you for being my friends. For understanding when I'm lost in a deadline, and for showing up every Monday for book binding regardless. Thank you for helping make hundreds of friendship bracelets, and dropping everything to help make a book signing possible. You guys keep me grounded and remind me life is bigger than my authorship and sometimes it's okay not to write...or abscond to the bookstore after a shady dice deal in a Walmart parking lot.

To the book community—

Holy hell, you guys never cease to blow me away with your kindness and support. I am always so nervous to put new books out in the world, and you always come clapping back, reminding me there is something for everyone and you love to take a chance on characters you love.

Every single time you tag me in a gorgeous photo or video I am reduced to giddy smiles and giggles. You seriously make my day and inspire me to fall in love with characters and keep telling emotionally charged stories.

And finally thank you to my readers.

Every. Single. One of you.

I wouldn't be here without you.

I am so grateful I get to do this job. Thank you for every sentence you read, every review you leave, every post you make. I see you. Thank you for taking a chance on me and my stories. You guys are magic.

xoxo

Hayden

ABOUT THE AUTHOR

Hayden is a California girl living in a North Carolina world…for now. After all, home is where the Army sends her husband next. When she isn't in the writing cave wrangling the voices in her head, you can find her soccer momming it up, enticing her two daughters into a game of Taco, Cat, Goat Cheese, Pizza, or enjoying the finer things in life like supporting her favorites sports teams with a frosty beverage in hand.

Stalk Hayden on her social media to find out what's coming up!

lockeandrivesbooks.com